"You're a very good liar."

Kelly's step faltered at Chase's words, her defenses going up like a brick wall. She'd felt so comfortable with Chase during the drive that she'd let herself forget he was in law enforcement.

She'd let herself become attracted to him.

Who was she trying to fool?

One of the reasons she'd asked him to team up with her had been that she was already attracted to him.

Far too much.

Dear Reader,

Is lying ever justified?

Kelly Carmichael thinks so, especially upon her
arrival in Indigo Springs when the truth could land
her back in jail. Then she meets and starts to fall
for Chase Bradford, who holds the opposite view—
and a badge.

That's the setup of *A Stranger's Sin,* the second book
in my Return to Indigo Springs trilogy. I thought it
would be interesting to pair a woman, who lies when
she has to, with a do-the-right-thing kind of guy and
see what happened.

Hint: there's a scene in the book during a Fourth of
July fireworks show.

All my best,

Darlene Gardner

P.S. Visit me on the Web at www.darlenegardner.com.

THE STRANGER'S SIN
Darlene Gardner

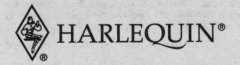

HARLEQUIN®

TORONTO • NEW YORK • LONDON
AMSTERDAM • PARIS • SYDNEY • HAMBURG
STOCKHOLM • ATHENS • TOKYO • MILAN • MADRID
PRAGUE • WARSAW • BUDAPEST • AUCKLAND

Recycling programs
for this product may
not exist in your area.

ISBN-13: 978-0-373-71562-6
ISBN-10:   0-373-71562-5

THE STRANGER'S SIN

Copyright © 2009 by Darlene Hrobak Gardner.

This edition published by arrangement with Harlequin Books S.A.

® and TM are trademarks of the publisher. Trademarks indicated with ® are registered in the United States Patent and Trademark Office, the Canadian Trade Marks Office and in other countries.

www.eHarlequin.com

Printed in U.S.A.

ABOUT THE AUTHOR

While working as a newspaper sportswriter, Darlene Gardner realized she'd rather make up quotes than rely on an athlete to say something interesting. So she quit her job and concentrated on a fiction career that landed her at Harlequin/Silhouette Books, where she wrote for Harlequin Temptation, Harlequin Duets and Silhouette Intimate Moments before finding a home at Harlequin Superromance.

Books by Darlene Gardner

HARLEQUIN SUPERROMANCE

*Return to Indigo Springs

Don't miss any of our special offers. Write to us at the following address for information on our newest releases.

Harlequin Reader Service
U.S.: 3010 Walden Ave., P.O. Box 1325, Buffalo, NY 14269
Canadian: P.O. Box 609, Fort Erie, Ont. L2A 5X3

To the truth, which has a way of coming out.

CHAPTER ONE

THE SWEET PROMISE OF FREEDOM lay just beyond the courthouse doors, a nearly irresistible proposition for a woman who'd spent the night in jail.

Kelly Carmichael longed to rush outside and turn her face to the late-June sun. The Wenona County courthouse was three or four miles from the cozy, one-bedroom town house in upstate New York where she lived alone. She planned to walk the entire way home, no matter how high the temperature climbed.

Then she'd take a long, cool shower. She yearned to wash away the horror of the eighteen hours since uniformed police officers had pounded on her door, shown her a warrant and taken her away in handcuffs.

But first she needed to hear what the attorney who'd represented her at the arraignment advised her to do about the colossal misunderstanding that had gotten her arrested.

The attorney stumbled out of the hall restroom, wiping the brow of his thin, pale face. She'd seen that same look of misery on one of her first-grade students last week. Spencer Yates, she guessed, had a stomach virus.

She rose from the wooden bench outside the court

clerk's window where her ex-boyfriend had posted her bail before leaving as quickly as he could. Spencer Yates was moving very slowly.

"Are you all right?" she asked.

"No, I am not all right," the lawyer snapped. His wisp of a moustache underscored how young he was, as though he couldn't yet grow decent facial hair. He put up a hand. "Sorry. It's just that this stomach thing has hit me pretty hard. So let's get down to it."

He indicated that she should precede him into a meeting room not much larger than the jail cell where she'd spent a sleepless Sunday night on a hard cot, counting down the hours until Monday's arraignment. He moved to pull the heavy door shut and last night's claustrophobia came rushing back.

"Please, can we leave the door open?" she asked, her voice cracking.

His hand dropped to his side. "Makes no difference to me."

He sat down heavily on one of the upholstered chairs alongside a meeting table with a laminate wood top and swiped a hand over his damp brow.

"Are you sure you're all right?" she asked.

"I'm fine," he said unconvincingly. "Even if I wasn't, we need to go over a few things."

He opened her file and removed some sheets of paper he'd had time only to glance at before the hearing. Kelly sat silently, trying to be patient. Yates had explained the district judge was interested in getting through his heavy load of arraignments rather than correcting mistakes.

But once the young lawyer looked over the specifics of her case, surely he'd see to it that justice was served.

In short order he put aside the papers, his head lolling slightly as though he had to put forth an effort to keep it up. "My suggestion is to see if the district attorney will go for a plea bargain. I'll try to get you a deal where you won't have to serve more than one year."

"One year! No!" She shook her head vigorously. Like mother, like daughter, she thought before her mind rebelled. "I can't go to prison. I won't."

He looked at her through tired eyes shadowed with heavy, dark circles. "You should have thought of that before the police found that baby at your place."

"But there's a perfectly good reason he was there." Kelly leaned forward, desperate to make him understand. She'd already told the story a dozen times in hours and hours of interrogation. "A woman I met on the playground asked me to babysit."

"Where is this woman?"

"I don't know where she is. I don't know anything about her except her name is Amanda Smith."

"So you agreed to babysit for a perfect stranger?" Yates put one elbow on the table and tiredly rested his chin in his hand. "The police aren't buying that story."

"It's the truth. Amanda has to be the one who kidnapped Corey."

"The baby's name is Eric, and the police think *you* kidnapped him. Right now you're facing charges of second-degree kidnapping, which is a felony. If the DA agrees, I might be able to get the charge reduced to endangering the welfare of a child. That's a misdemeanor."

Misdemeanor sounded better than *felony,* but the words still sent dread coursing through her. If she pleaded guilty to either of those charges, she'd have a permanent criminal record and the repercussions that came with it. "If I'm convicted, nobody will ever hire me to teach again!"

He stared at her as though it was of little importance to him whether she lost her job as a first-grade teacher.

"You don't understand," she said. "Teaching children is all I've ever wanted to do."

"Yeah, well, maybe you're not the sort of person who should be around kids."

It took a few seconds for his meaning to sink in. A shudder raked her from head to toe. "You think I'm guilty, don't you?"

"I shouldn't have said that." He rubbed the back of his neck. "But it doesn't matter whether I think you're guilty or not. What matters is whether there's enough evidence here to win at trial. And there's not."

"I don't believe you," she said.

He opened his eyes the rest of the way and straightened his backbone. "If you're not satisfied with my counsel, you can request to be reassigned to another lawyer. With the overwhelming evidence against you, though, another lawyer will tell you the same thing."

"What overwhelming evidence?"

"Besides the kidnapped baby the police found in your town house? The report says you spend hours watching children at the playground."

"I don't go alone," she countered. "My next-door

neighbor runs a business out of her home. I take her son to the playground to help her out."

"Okay, then. How about the fact that the person who called the police after hearing the Amber Alert said you're unhappy you can't have children of your own?"

"Of course I am! What woman wouldn't be?" she cried. She was sorry she'd ever shared that sad information with any of the women at the playground. "That's not proof."

"The baby was taken from a stroller outside a grocery store in Utica on Friday night." He named a town in New York about an hour away and tapped her file folder, which he'd already closed. "On Sunday the police found that baby with you."

"I wasn't in Utica!"

A spark of interest lit his eyes. "Can anyone verify that?"

Kelly thought back to the thriller that had kept her reading Friday night until the last page. Too bad fictional characters couldn't give alibis. "No," she admitted.

His eyes went flat again. "There are two eyewitnesses who described the suspect as a woman in her twenties of average height and weight with shoulder-length brown hair.

"That could describe a lot of women," Kelly said, even as panic started to set in. She couldn't deny she and the woman at the playground shared a resemblance.

"One of the eyewitnesses picked you out of a photo lineup," he said. "Do you see the problem here? A jury will believe you're guilty. We'll be lucky if we do get a plea, but it would certainly come with a stipulation that you submit to counseling. If we didn't take it, you could be facing up to eight years."

She swallowed her panic, making herself think, picking out the hole in his argument. "If the evidence is so overwhelming, why did the judge grant me bail?"

"Quite frankly, given the nature of the crime, it surprised me that he did." He gestured with his hand. "Who knows? It could be because you have ties in the community and no priors. And bail was high enough he probably thought you couldn't make it."

She understood how the judge could believe a defendant who needed a court-appointed attorney wouldn't have the money to cover the huge amount set for bail. Or even the ten percent a bail bondsman charged. "A friend posted bail for me."

Yates quirked an eyebrow, but didn't ask what sort of friend coughed up that kind of money. His face was growing paler by the second. He clearly didn't want to hear about her relationship with Vince Dawkins, who'd materialized at the arraignment like a benevolent ghost.

Kelly would have preferred not to accept favors from Vince, who worked as a reading resource teacher at the private Edgerton School where she also taught, but the alternative was going back to jail and she'd been desperate.

Vince was wealthy enough that the bail amount would be a trifle for him. Besides, he still felt guilty for the way their relationship had ended.

"Just be thankful you caught Judge Waters in a good mood," Yates said, "because he's usually much harsher on people conventional wisdom says are flight risks."

The lawyer couldn't be serious. Kelly Carmichael, a

flight risk? Despite her mother's long rap sheet, Kelly had never tangled with the law until yesterday. She'd spent the last two years establishing herself in the community with a town house she'd turned into a home and a career she loved.

A career that, according to Spencer Yates, was in serious jeopardy. She was working as a counselor at the Edgerton School's summer camp, a position she'd already lost. Vince had informed her the school's principal said she shouldn't come back until this matter was cleared up.

"I'll give you a call after I talk with the DA." Yates stood, swaying slightly on his feet. He acted as though the matter was all settled, as though she'd agreed to let him work out a deal that would send her to prison.

"But—"

"I really need to go." Yates turned even more gray. He hurried out of the meeting room, calling over his shoulder, "You have my number if you need me."

She stared after him, frustrated because she had so much more to say. But Yates was clearly ill—and as disinterested in hearing about the woman at the playground as the police had been. If Kelly retained him as her lawyer, he'd get around to asking the same tough question the police had: Why had nobody else seen the woman?

The reason was both simple and complicated.

Nobody had seen her because Kelly had been the only one at the playground. Late on a Saturday afternoon. Without her neighbor's two-year-old son.

Kelly hadn't set out to visit the playground. Her intention had been to enjoy the beautiful summer weather.

Her walk took her past the swings and the monkey bars, the place where she spent so many happy hours. The woman—she'd given her name only as Amanda Smith— had been trying to get her baby boy to stop crying. Kelly's first mistake had been stopping to talk to her.

Kelly shook off the memory and stood up, suddenly desperate to be outdoors. She hurried out of the courthouse and into the brightness of the summer morning. She gazed up into the cloudless blue sky, watching the flight of a hawk that was free to go wherever it pleased.

So was she, but not for long. The police weren't searching for the real kidnapper. Kelly was headed for prison unless…

Unless she found Amanda herself.

The idea took root and sprouted. It was crazy, but it was her only option.

There was the not-so-minor detail that she wasn't allowed to leave the state of New York under the terms of her bail, but if she was back before her next scheduled court appearance, Vince might not even lose the money he'd posted for her bail. If she wasn't, she'd find a way to pay him back, even if it meant selling her town house.

But she couldn't think about that now. She needed to remember something—anything—Amanda might have said that would provide a clue on where to look.

Their conversation had revolved around the baby. Amanda hadn't talked about where she'd grown up or where she lived but it seemed to Kelly she had mentioned a place.

Yes. That was right. She'd said something about there being no more to do in Wenona than in…what? The name of the town floated in Kelly's brain, just out of reach of her consciousness.

Green Water? No. That was wrong. It hadn't been Water, it had been…Springs. But Green Springs wasn't right. Neither was Blue Springs.

Indigo Springs.

The name hit her with such certainty that she rushed down the courthouse steps, eager to get to a computer so she could figure out where Indigo Springs was.

Because that's where she was headed.

CHAPTER TWO

CHASE BRADFORD SET DOWN the car seat that doubled as a carrier, acting as if it made perfect sense for the invited guest at the Indigo Springs library's Summer Speaker Series to bring along a sleeping year-old baby.

"Dream on, buddy," he whispered, squashing an urge to kiss one of Toby's flushed, chubby cheeks. "Please, please dream on."

He wouldn't have called himself soft-hearted before Toby came into his life, but it had taken Chase about ten seconds flat to fall in love with the little guy.

He'd fallen pretty quickly for Toby's mother, too, but that turned out to have nothing to do with love. He wasn't usually impulsive when it came to women. After Mandy, he wouldn't be again.

"You sure that baby will be okay there?" asked Louise Wiesneski, the big-boned, florid-faced librarian who'd set up the talk.

"He'll be fine, Louise," Chase said with more confidence than he felt.

Her eyebrows formed an inverted V and her mouth twisted. "If you say so."

She turned to the small group of people milling about

the meeting room. Chase recognized a few faces, but the group consisted mostly of the outdoor enthusiasts who descended on the town in summer to hike, bike and ride the white water down the Lehigh River.

"Please take a seat," she commanded. "We're about to start."

The people who weren't yet seated pulled chairs out from the tables facing the front of the room, the legs scraping on the linoleum floor.

Toby promptly woke up, his baby blues opening wide.

His tiny face crumpled, he kicked his short legs and he opened his little mouth. Chase bent down before he could scream, filling the baby's field of vision with his familiar face. Toby closed his mouth, his lips forming into a pout, and stretched out both arms.

As timing went, Toby's couldn't have been worse.

Unbuckling the baby from the carrier, Chase resigned himself to having a partner during his presentation. He picked up Toby, smoothing his blond hair back from his flushed face, hoping the baby would be a silent partner.

A few dozen faces stared up at him while he said a silent prayer of thanks that he hadn't opted for a slide show. The way things were going, he'd have a hard enough time passing around the oversize photos he'd brought along.

"Tonight we have Chase Bradford, a wildlife conservation officer whose talk is titled: 'That Wasn't a Mountain Lion.'" Louise's voice sounded amplified even without a microphone. "Chase will speak about some of the species of wildlife that can be spotted in the Poconos."

Doing his best to pretend he didn't have a baby in his

arms, Chase held up a photo of a man kneeling beside a large, dead animal. "Can anybody tell me what this is?"

The hand of a freckled-faced boy sitting in the front row shot up. He was no older than ten, the youngest person in the room. Before Chase could acknowledge him, the boy asked, "Are you a policeman?"

"Not exactly," he said just as Toby covered his badge with a chubby hand. "Think of me as policing the woods and waters. I help hunters, fishermen and outdoor enthusiasts enjoy our state's resources responsibly."

Chase repositioned Toby and asked again, "Now does anybody have a guess about this animal?"

"It's a mountain lion," answered a man wearing hiking clothing and a sunburn.

"That's right," Chase said. "A big one, too. Probably somewhere in the two-hundred-pound range. So now you're probably wondering about the title of my talk."

Toby squirmed, obviously still out of sorts from being awakened so abruptly. The baby almost never napped in the early evening but had fallen asleep on the drive over. His routine was seriously messed up.

"This photo made the rounds on the Internet a while back, with the text claiming the animal had been hit by a truck in a number of locations, including right here in Pennsylvania."

Toby whimpered, and Chase bounced the baby the way he'd seen mothers calm their fussy children. Unfortunately motion wasn't usually the key to soothing Toby. The baby was the ultimate outdoors enthusiast. Take him outside and he instantly quieted.

Louise crossed her arms over her chest, her lips flatlining.

"But there are no mountain lions in Pennsylvania and haven't been since the late 1800s," Chase said just as Toby let out a lusty wail. He bounced the baby some more, with no success. "This big cat was killed in northern Arizona."

The volume of Toby's cries increased. The freckled-faced boy in the front row covered his ears.

"Over the years, people have claimed mountain lions are roaming our hills." Chase spoke louder to be heard above Toby's cries. "But then some Pennsylvanians also claim to have seen Sasquatch."

Nobody laughed.

Louise straightened from where she'd been leaning against the wall, marched over to Chase and held out her arms. "I'll take him."

Chase's grip on the baby tightened, but he couldn't continue the presentation over Toby's howls. "Sorry about this. He'll calm down if you take him outside."

He had a moment's doubt before handing the baby over, but the librarian's entire body softened when she took him. She headed for the door, whispering soothing words, and Chase relaxed.

The freckled boy's hand raised, bringing Chase's attention back to the group. "Do you bring your baby on patrol, too?"

Considering its inauspicious beginning, the talk went over well. Chase showed the group photos of black bears, coyotes, red foxes and bobcats. The young boy was particularly interested in what Chase had to say about timber rattlers and copperheads, which was basically "Poison—stay away."

The talk finally over, Chase picked up the baby carrier and went in search of Toby and the librarian. He found them on the sidewalk outside the library, with Louise balancing the baby on her hip as she pointed out the things around them in a soft, pleasant voice.

Sky. Tree. Grass. Bench.

"We just finished up," Chase said as he walked toward them. "Thanks for watching Toby for me, Louise."

The librarian's demeanor instantly changed, her whole body turning rigid and uncompromising. She handed Toby over, but not before Chase saw her press a quick, furtive kiss to the back of the baby's head.

"What were you thinking bringing a baby with you?" she demanded.

He was thinking he needed to talk his retired father into carrying a cell phone. Then he could have reminded him of his promise to babysit.

"My dad and I got our signals crossed." Chase should have mentioned the talk when he got home from work, but figured whatever errand his father needed to run wouldn't take long. He'd figured wrong.

"Your dad?" Her voice had a hard, suspicious edge. "Isn't he a widower?"

How had she known that? Tourism had arrived in Indigo Springs years before Chase's parents bought the vacation home where Chase now lived with his father. While Indigo Springs still had a small-town feel, it wasn't so insular that residents automatically knew everyone else's business.

"Yes, he is." Chase bent to lower Toby into the carrier and started buckling him in, making sure the straps went over the baby's shoulders and between his legs. "My mother died nine months ago."

"I was sorry to hear about that," she mumbled, then added in a clearer voice, "So if your father's watching Toby for you, that must mean Mandy's still out of town."

Chase looked up at her sharply at the mention of Toby's mother. "How do you know Mandy?"

"She was a regular at the library. She mentioned once she was living with a wildlife conservation officer. That's how I got the idea to ask you to speak."

Chase turned back to Toby and finished buckling the gurgling baby into the carrier. He squashed an impulse to demand Louise immediately tell him what she knew about Mandy. Picking up the carrier by its sturdy plastic handle, he forced himself to sound casual.

"Were you and Mandy friends?"

"Oh, no," the librarian said. "She just came in here to read her magazines—*People, Vogue, Cosmo.* Never touched *Parents* magazine or *American Baby,* though she had this little one and told one of the other librarians she was pregnant. She had a miscarriage, didn't she?"

Chase kept his expression stoic, determined that Louise not guess she'd hit on a sore spot. "Yeah, she did."

"Wasn't that about three weeks ago?" Louise didn't wait for confirmation, suggesting she'd been downwind from some serious gossip. "I heard she left town right after. Where did she go anyway?"

That was the million-dollar question.

"Nowhere in particular," he said carefully. "She just needed to get away."

"From her baby?" Louise arched a skeptical eyebrow. "When will she be back?"

Chase nearly told her to mind her own business, but she clearly liked to gossip. Since she was bound to give her co-workers a cry-by-cry account of tonight's bring-a-baby-to-work fiasco, it would be best not to alienate her.

"Soon," he said.

"I certainly hope so," she said. "A baby needs his mother."

In Toby's case, Chase disagreed.

Toby uttered some gibberish, awarding Chase with one of his priceless grins.

"Thanks again for having me," he told Louise, "but I need to get this happy little guy home so I can get him to bed on time."

He felt like a politician on the campaign trail, putting the best possible spin on a situation after getting called for a misstep. Damage control, the politicians called it.

He headed for his Jeep before she could ask another question. He'd been facing more and more of them lately, most dealing with whether he and his father were equipped to handle a baby.

It was only a matter of time before somebody guessed that Chase didn't have a clue where Mandy had gone.

Or whether she was ever coming back.

THE GLOW OF THE microwave brightened the dark side of the kitchen; Chase hadn't bothered to turn on a light.

He waited for the shrill beep, then opened the microwave door, noting the time on the digital display.

Eleven fifty-six, a good three hours since he'd put Toby down for the night and at least an hour since Chase had turned out his own bedside light.

He'd switched it back on again a few minutes ago.

He removed the mug from the microwave, his eyes drifting to the whiteboard affixed to the side of the refrigerator. It was too dark to read the lines his father had scribbled in black marker but he knew them by heart.

Don't worry. Home late.

The mystery of where his early-to-bed father had gone paled only in comparison to Mandy's disappearing act.

Chase heard the mechanical sound of the garage door raising, signaling that he'd soon find out the answer to at least one of the puzzles.

"Hi, Dad," he said when his father walked into the kitchen a few moments later.

His father's body jerked, then relaxed. A tall man with a full head of gray hair, he'd nearly shattered when his wife died but lately Chase had seen signs that he was coming back to life. Not only had he gone out tonight, but he'd taken care with his appearance, wearing a new-looking short-sleeved polo shirt with his favorite khakis.

"I didn't see you there." Charlie Bradford carried his shoes in one hand, as though afraid the click of his heels on the hardwood would wake up the household. "I thought you'd be asleep."

Chase held up his mug. "I'm trying Mom's remedy."

"Ah, warm milk," his father said.

Chase brought the mug to his lips, blew on the liquid and took a sip. The thick, chalky taste filled his mouth, and he made a face. "Ugh. As terrible as ever."

His father chuckled softly. "I never could stand the stuff. Always thought it was better to talk about what's keeping you up."

"Is it that obvious?"

"Asked the man drinking warm milk in the middle of summer," his father quipped.

Chase set the mug down on the kitchen counter. "It's Toby."

"Is he all right?" his father asked sharply.

"He's fine," Chase assured him, "but I've been thinking about that message Mandy left on my cell phone."

Chase had received the voice mail a few days after he discovered her "miscarriage" was a convenient way to explain away a pregnancy that had never been, not that he'd shared that embarrassing tidbit with his father or anyone else.

He'd met Mandy Smith at the tail end of a year he'd been in Harrisburg attending training school to become a Pennsylvania Game Commission employee. After his March graduation, he'd been assigned a territory that included Indigo Springs. Weeks later, she'd phoned to tell him their single night together had resulted in pregnancy.

What else could he do but invite her to live with him? Had the pregnancy progressed, he would have asked her to marry him. It would have been the right thing to do. Instead he'd been played for a fool.

In the voice mail Mandy had rambled on about leaving Toby, but explained that she wasn't cut out to be a mother.

"I don't think she's coming back for him," Chase said.

"That could be," his father said. "That girl wasn't much of a mother."

His father should know. During the two months Mandy had lived with them in Indigo Springs, his dad had spent more time with Toby than Mandy had.

Chase drew in a breath, then put into words the conclusion he'd reached while lying in bed. "I need to contact the Department of Public Welfare."

"No! That's a terrible idea," his father cried. "Where's this coming from? Did something happen tonight?"

"Yes and no," Chase said. "It's just that the librarian who set up my speech asked a lot of questions."

His father put a hand to his head and groaned, then sank into a chair beside Chase. "I forgot about your speech."

"Yeah, you did."

"You don't usually need me on your day off, but I still should have remembered." He grimaced. "You had to take Toby with you, didn't you?"

"I tried some of the neighbors but nobody could watch him," Chase said.

"How was he?"

"Noisy. The librarian took him outside for me, then she quizzed me about Mandy. Turns out Mandy used to come into the library to read magazines."

"I'm sorry," his father said, but still didn't offer an explanation for where he'd been. Odd. His father had to know Chase wanted him to get out of the house and go somewhere besides the river with his fishing pole.

"Where were you anyway?" Chase asked finally.

"Nowhere special." His father added hurriedly, "Why would some librarian asking questions about Toby make you think you have to go to DPW?"

Chase opted not to repeat the question he'd asked his strangely secretive father. "Because she's not the only one. Mandy's been gone for almost three weeks. Sooner or later, someone will figure out we don't have legal custody."

"We won't have legal custody if you go to DPW, either," his father pointed out. "The agency would."

"Yeah," Chase said, "but it's the right thing to do."

"The right thing to do," his father muttered, running a hand over his lower face. "You're just like your mother. She was always going on about right and wrong, as though it was easy to see the difference."

"It is easy," Chase said.

"Not true. What if DPW takes Toby away from us? Think about it, Chase. You work long, unpredictable hours, and I'm sixty-seven years old. Toby's a normal, healthy baby. Do you know how many couples out there are looking to adopt a baby like him?"

"Toby's not up for adoption, Dad. I'm thinking we could ask to be his foster parents. He's lived with us for two months. It wouldn't make sense to move him."

His father's head shook vehemently. "It's too much of a risk. There's no way you can know for sure that DPW wouldn't take Toby away from us."

That possibility was what had driven Chase to the kitchen in search of the warm milk he couldn't drink.

If Louise Wiesneski were a social worker instead of a librarian, Chase doubted she'd let Toby continue to live with him and his father. She clearly didn't think much of his parenting ability.

"I know you want to do the right thing, but look at it this way," his father continued. "The right thing for Toby is to stay with us."

"We can't just keep him indefinitely, Dad," Chase said. "Sooner or later, I need to go to the authorities."

"Then make it later. Three weeks is too soon to be sure she isn't coming back."

"It's getting there."

"Okay, then let's say she isn't coming back. Mandy told you she didn't have any family, right? That means she left Toby for you to raise. So find her and get her to give you custody."

After his father went to sleep, Chase sat at the kitchen table, his hands cradling the now-cooled milk, trying to figure out what to do.

Find her, his father had advised.

The directive wasn't nearly as easy as it should have been. He'd made a couple of stabs at it already, but he had no credit-card information to trace or phone numbers to track down. He'd checked his phone bills and Mandy hadn't made any long-distance calls while she was living with him. He'd even taken a short trip to Harrisburg, but the employees of the bar where they'd met claimed not to know her. The clerk at the hotel where she'd rented a room said she'd paid in cash.

Looking back on it, Mandy had been closemouthed about her past and Chase hadn't spent much time getting her to open up. He'd been too busy trying to get along with her.

So how could he go about finding a woman he didn't know anything about?

CHAPTER THREE

INDIGO SPRINGS TURNED OUT to be a picturesque town in the Pocono Mountains, with charming stone buildings lining a hilly main street that provided stunning views of the surrounding area.

The lush green of the valley mingled with the majesty of the mountains and the blue backdrop of the sky. Kelly would have felt as if she'd been transported to the pages of a storybook if she hadn't been searching for the only person who could keep her out of prison.

The clerk behind the counter at the busy ice-cream shop shook her head and tried to give the color sketch Kelly had done of Amanda back to her.

"Are you sure she's not at least a little familiar?" Kelly shifted her heavy backpack, repeating the same question she'd used on the string of clerks and receptionists in the stores along the town's main street. "It's not a perfect likeness."

"I'll be glad to look at it again." The clerk had a matronly figure and a round, pleasant face, with big eyes that narrowed when she concentrated. After a few moments, she muttered, "Come to think of it, something about her does seem familiar."

Kelly's heart gave a hopeful leap. Finally, after hours of frustration, this could be the break she'd been waiting for. She held her breath as though even the simple act of exhaling might ruin the clerk's concentration. Time seemed to lengthen, and the swirl of conversation dimmed, taking a back seat to the drama.

"I've got it!" the clerk said decisively. Her gaze lifted. "She looks like you."

The air left Kelly's lungs, the hope that her long shot was about to pay off fading along with it. This wasn't the first time today Kelly had experienced the same swing of emotions. A half dozen other people had also pointed out the resemblance. Kelly was beginning to understand how the eyewitness had mistakenly picked her out of a photo lineup.

"It's not me." Kelly took back the sketch. "But thanks for looking at it."

"Well, I hope you find her," the clerk said kindly. "Do you mind me asking why you're searching for her?"

"I have something of hers," Kelly said. Before she could expand on her answer, the door banged open, admitting a noisy, laughing family of four.

"I want chocolate chip." The smaller of the two children, a thin, dark-haired girl of about three years old, skipped up to the counter, flashing an adorable smile. Her mother immediately followed, placing hands on the girl's shoulders to hold her back.

"You have to wait your turn, sweetie," she said.

"Why?" the girl asked, eyes big and wide.

As the mother explained, the clerk laughed, then told Kelly, "We've been really busy this week with the

Fourth of July weekend coming up. Can I get you something?"

Why not? Kelly thought, and ordered a bowl of fudge ripple ice cream. She found a table at the back of the store, shrugged off the backpack and sat down, digging into the ice cream with a plastic spoon while people laughed and talked all around her.

It didn't dawn on her how hungry she was until she swallowed the first mouthful. The last thing she'd eaten was a package of cheese crackers from a vending machine. When had that been? This morning? Last night?

She truly didn't remember. Driving her own car to Indigo Springs had seemed too risky, so the Tuesday morning after her Monday arraignment she'd set out for the bus station. Using cash she'd withdrawn from her modest savings account, she'd taken a series of buses. What would have been a five-hour trip had stretched to eighteen, with Kelly trying to catch snatches of sleep during the long night of transfers and layovers.

It occurred to her that by covering her tracks she was acting like a guilty woman. At the very least, she'd violated the terms of her bail, but she didn't see how the authorities would know she was gone until she failed to show up for her preliminary hearing, whenever that was. Spencer Yates, if he suspected she'd left the state, should be bound by attorney-client privilege not to tell.

In any event, she couldn't go back to Wenona until she found Amanda, and that might take a while. Nobody who'd seen the sketch had inspired even a glimmer of hope, with the exception of the construction worker with the great smile.

It turned out he hadn't recognized Amanda, either, which wasn't surprising. He'd been supervising the construction of a new wing of town hall, his attention divided between a crew putting up drywall and a desperate woman shoving a sketch at him.

She gazed down at her bowl, stunned that it was already empty. Weariness set in from her nearly sleepless night, weighing down her very bones. She needed to summon the energy to pick up the backpack she'd stuffed full of clothes and leave the ice-cream shop. She had only a few more businesses to canvas. Once she did, she'd have to tax her tired brain to come up with a new strategy.

She supposed she could make copies of the sketch and hand them out on the street, but she'd have to include contact information, something she was reluctant to do because she couldn't shake the feeling the authorities would be looking for her.

The jingling of the bell on the door announcing the arrival of a new customer added to the general hubbub. Kelly looked up, expecting more tourists in search of an afternoon snack.

A tall man in a policeman's uniform entered the shop. He ignored the ice-cream counter, his gaze sweeping the shop and zeroing in on Kelly. The breath in her chest froze, as cold as the ice cream she'd just eaten. She told herself to remain calm, and reminded herself she'd only left Wenona yesterday. The law couldn't possibly have found her already. Even her attorney couldn't be sure she was gone.

The cop played havoc with her rationale, striding directly for her. Her heart stampeded, and she felt like she might pass out.

The penalty for violating the conditions of bail was an immediate return to jail. She imagined herself behind bars, heard the sound of a cell door slamming shut, felt the weight of panic crushing her chest.

He stopped at her table and loomed over her, blotting out her view of everything but him. "I need to talk to you."

Battling her growing dread, she tipped her chin, fervently reminding herself she was innocent. "I didn't do anything wrong."

The corners of the cop's mouth dipped slightly. "I didn't say you did."

"Then why…" She stopped in midquestion, belatedly realizing his uniform of a short-sleeved khaki shirt and dark pants was decidedly different than those worn by the New York policemen who'd arrested her. "You're not a cop, are you?"

"No," he said.

She squinted, making out the words on his silver badge. *Wildlife Conservation Officer* it read. Another term for forest ranger.

Relief saturated her limbs, making them weak. Her brain started to function with more clarity. Even in the unlikely event the cops in New York knew she'd left the state, this was Pennsylvania. If this man had been a cop, he wouldn't be on the lookout for her.

"Would it matter if I *was* a cop?" He had an aggressively masculine face with a square jaw, lean cheeks and an outdoorsman's tan. Short, thick brown hair, lightened

by the sun, sprang back from a widow's peak above as-
sessing brown eyes. She guessed he wasn't yet thirty.

"No. No. Of course not." She bit her lip to stop from
issuing another denial. She tried to smile but felt her lips
quiver. "What did you want to talk to me about?"

He gestured to the sketch on the tabletop. "That," he
said. "Can I sit down?"

"Yes, of course." She felt like she was on a roller
coaster, having survived one plunge only to be ascend-
ing another incline, praying this one wasn't too tall to
climb. She turned the sketch around so that it faced him.
"Do you know her?"

He picked up the paper, his expression giving away
nothing. She wondered who had told him about the
sketch. Her guess was the construction worker, who'd
probably known more than he was telling.

"I might," he said. "What's her name?"

"Amanda Smith."

He gave no indication he recognized the name. "Why
are you looking for her?"

"I have something she'd want back." She unzipped
an outer pocket of her backpack and pulled out a necklace. Fake gemstones of jade, lapis and ruby hung from
a thick gold herringbone chain that looked just like
fourteen-karat gold. "It's costume jewelry, but it's
vintage. This one's exceptionally pretty."

"Did she give it to you?" he asked.

"Oh, no. I don't know her nearly well enough for
that. In fact, I don't know her at all." She was letting his
direct gaze disconcert her, and as a result she was almost
babbling. She made herself stop.

"Then how did you know to come to Indigo Springs?" he asked.

She regrouped, calling to mind the story she'd concocted on the bus. "She mentioned the town after we shared a table at a really crowded coffee shop. After she left, I found the necklace. The clasp is broken."

Only the last part was true. She'd found the necklace in the kidnapped baby's carrier and theorized the baby had tugged it loose. She wasn't sure whether the necklace belonged to Amanda or the kidnapped baby's mother, but it provided a convenient cover story.

"Where was this coffee shop?" the forest ranger asked.

The other people who'd heard the story had taken it at face value, asking few follow-up questions. She groped for an answer that would be general enough.

"Upstate New York."

"Really?" He put down the sketch, rested his forearms on the table and leaned forward, his eyes still fastened on hers. "So you drove all the way to Pennsylvania from upstate New York to return a piece of costume jewelry?"

Stated that way, her story sounded ridiculous and unbelievable. She clasped her hands, feeling sweat on her palms. She made sure to meet his eyes so he wouldn't know for certain that she was lying. "Oh, no. I happened to be passing through."

"With a sketch?"

She bit her lower lip so the truth wouldn't come tumbling out. Her intuition told her the forest ranger could be trusted, but her instincts had failed her in a catastrophic way when she'd run across Amanda and the baby. It wasn't difficult to understood why the cops had a hard time believing she'd agreed to babysit for a stranger.

This man was as much an unknown as Amanda had been. She didn't need to justify herself. Kelly tapped the sketch with her index finger. "Do you know her or don't you?"

"Not as a brunette, as a redhead." He straightened but kept watching her just as closely. "I have some photos of her I can show you."

Adrenaline coursed through Kelly. It made sense that a woman who kidnapped a child might also disguise her appearance. She couldn't keep the eagerness from her voice. "Where is she now?"

"If I knew that, I wouldn't be sitting here," he said.

A static-filled voice suddenly came over his two-way radio. He pulled the device from his belt, uttering a quick, "Excuse me. I have to take this."

The man at the other end of the line said something about a black bear rooting through garbage at a campsite. The forest ranger listened, nodding, frustration chasing across his features. He signed off.

"We'll have to continue this later," he said. "Are you staying in town?"

Now that she'd stumbled across a lead, she would be. "Yes. When can you meet me?"

He glanced at the clock on the wall, which showed it was already past three. "How about seven o'clock? My place. I'll show you those photos."

He reached into his wallet, pulled out a card and handed it to her. *Chase Bradford. Pennsylvania Game Commission.* "That's my home address and telephone number. Do you have a card? A number where I can reach you?"

She didn't dare give him her cell-phone number and she hadn't yet checked into a hotel. It seemed likely that a forest ranger would have contacts in the law-enforcement community with access to information databases. He had no reason to investigate her now, but she needed to think ahead and be smart.

"I don't have a cell phone," she lied, "but I'll be at your house at seven."

He appeared reluctant to leave her, but she sensed he was a man who didn't shirk his duties. "I didn't catch your name."

"Kelly," she answered automatically before her newfound sense of self-preservation kicked in. "Kelly Delaney."

"Where are you from, Kelly?"

Kelly Carmichael was from Wenona, New York. Kelly Delaney, who happened to be a college friend who shared her first name and had also majored in education, wasn't. She dredged up the name of her friend's hometown from the Christmas cards they still exchanged. "Schenectady."

If the forest ranger got suspicious and had a friend run Kelly Delaney's name, he wouldn't find anything to sound alarm bells.

"I'll see you tonight, Kelly Delaney."

After he left the shop, her shoulders drooped and she cradled her head in her hands. She prayed that Chase Bradford would have information that would lead her to Amanda.

Because now, in the eyes of the law, Kelly wasn't only an accused criminal.

She was a fugitive with an alias.

KELLY HEARD THE CRIES before she spotted the woman. She sat on a park bench adjacent to a deserted playground, a baby in her arms.

The gray clouds, heavy with the threat of rain, had kept the regulars away. No children scampered up the stairs to the clubhouse or swung from the swings. There was just the lone woman and the baby.

"Shut up!" The woman's voice, rich with frustration, carried on the breeze. "I can't take it anymore! Why won't you stop crying?"

Kelly didn't hesitate. She veered from the path, toward the playground, walking at a fast clip. "Excuse me, but can I help?"

The woman turned around. She was an attractive brunette about Kelly's age with tears streaking down her cheeks. Lines of strain bracketed her mouth and creased her forehead.

"Oh, yes." She stood up and held out the baby. "Could you hold him for just a minute?"

It was a baby boy about three or four months old with blue eyes and light-blond hair, his face red from crying. Kelly's heart melted. She held out her arms for the baby. "Sure."

The sky darkened and thunder rumbled, followed by loud voices, one male, one female.

"Where do you want to go to dinner?"

"That Italian place on the corner looked good."

Kelly frowned, trying to figure out what the man and woman were doing in the park. Where had they come from? And why couldn't she see them? For that matter, where was the baby and the woman who couldn't stand his crying? What had happened to the park? All she saw now was blackness.

Realization dawned, and her eyes snapped open. She wasn't in a park in Wenona at all, but in a room with the shades pulled down, lying on a feather mattress.

She'd been dreaming about stumbling across Amanda and Corey—no, not Corey. The kidnapped baby's real name was Eric—on that fateful day she'd tried to help out a stranger. If the dream had continued, she would have seen herself agreeing to babysit for a few hours until Amanda pulled herself together.

A dream. It had only been a dream. As she struggled to come more fully awake, she dredged up the past few hours.

Wandering through Indigo Springs looking for a room, which had proved to be a tough task with the Fourth of July just three days away.

Checking into a room she really couldn't afford at the Blue Stream Bed-and-Breakfast.

Phoning her home answering machine to discover Spencer Yates was still trying to work out a deal with the DA and the judge had scheduled a preliminary hearing nine days from today.

Falling asleep on top of the comforter.

The noise she'd heard hadn't been thunder but some of the other guests descending the wooden stairs outside her room. But it shouldn't be dinnertime yet. Amanda had lain down around four-thirty, setting the alarm on her cell phone to wake her up at five-thirty so she had time to get ready and eat something before meeting Chase Bradford.

She turned her head, catching a glimpse of the time on the bedside clock: seven-fifteen.

She bolted to a sitting position, shoving the hair back from her face, swinging her legs over the side of the bed.

The alarm must not have gone off.

She dashed for the bathroom, grateful that the room came with a private one, splashed water on her face and peered at herself in the mirror. With smudges of mascara under her eyes, her clothes wrinkled and her hair sticking up in all directions, she looked a fright, like the kind of crazy woman who might actually snatch a baby.

It wasn't the kind of image she should present to Chase Bradford.

She turned on the shower and stripped out of her clothes. She hated being late for the meeting, but she could call him from the phone in the hall once she was presentable. She'd shown Chase's business card to the desk clerk who'd checked her in so she already had directions.

The talkative clerk knew Chase because she volunteered in the church nursery during Sunday services and he had a little boy he sometimes left there. The clerk knew Mandy, the boy's mother, less well but had let it slip that Mandy had moved in with Chase when she got pregnant.

Fighting a ridiculous wave of disappointment that Chase was either married or at the very least romantically involved with Mandy, she stepped into the shower. She wasn't sure why it mattered except that Chase had seemed solid and dependable, the kind of man who'd see through a woman like Amanda.

But she was jumping ahead of herself. She wasn't yet sure that Amanda and Mandy were the same woman. She'd assumed Amanda was childless because it seemed far-fetched that a mother would kidnap a baby. But then nothing about the devastating events of the past few days made sense. If Chase was involved with the woman who'd perpetrated the crime, that would be good news. Surely he'd have some ideas about where she might have gone.

As the water streamed down on Kelly and grew cold, a chilling question occurred to her. If Kelly was on the right track and Chase found out the real reason Kelly was searching for Amanda/Mandy, which woman would he be more likely to believe was guilty of kidnapping?

The woman who was mother to his son, or a complete stranger?

CHASE'S FATHER PACED TO the bay window that overlooked the street and peered into the twilight, a journey he'd been taking with increasing regularity.

"She's already an hour late." He stated a fact of which Chase was only too aware. "Think she stood you up?"

"It's starting to look that way," Chase admitted, internally kicking himself for the way he'd handled his first meeting with Kelly Delaney. He'd sensed she wasn't being completely honest but had failed to ask where in town she was staying. Tracking her down wouldn't be that difficult—if she was still in Indigo Springs.

It had been pure bad luck to get called away on that

nuisance-black-bear call before he got any useful information but he hadn't anticipated her not showing.

Any woman who'd go to the trouble of drawing a sketch and showing it around town had seemed a good bet to follow through on her search.

"Maybe she figured out she was looking for a different woman," his father theorized.

Chase shook his head. "I don't think so, Dad. She has a necklace I remember Mandy wearing. Although I've got to admit it seems strange for her to go to all this trouble to give it back."

"Not so strange. Some people are good Samaritans. She could be one of them." His father's voice caught on the last word and he groaned, his face turning pale.

"Dad, are you all right?" Chase asked. His father hadn't seemed well all night, but had waved off Chase's earlier concerns, claiming he'd overdone the yard work.

His father swallowed, seemed to take stock of himself, then nodded. "Yeah, I'm fine. Must have been a cramp. I'm sure it's nothing to worry about."

"Ba, Ba," Toby cried, distracting Chase from his father's problem. The baby sat on the floor in the middle of the room, his face creased with delight as he patted a large colorful ball. The ball rolled away. He giggled, crawling after it as fast as his chubby knees would carry him.

"You almost got it, bud," Chase's father called, seeming like his old self again. "Keep on going."

Toby reached the ball and batted at it, only to have it roll farther away. He laughed wildly, with Chase and his father joining in.

It was a simple moment, not unlike a thousand others since Toby had come to live with them.

It brought home how much Chase needed to find Mandy so he could get legal custody of the boy he already loved as a son. He shouldn't have made the mistake of assuming Kelly Delaney was as desperate to locate her as he was.

The doorbell rang, surprising them both. His father had kept such a close watch on the window, he would have seen headlights had a car pulled up.

Figuring their caller was most likely a neighbor, Chase went to the door and pulled it open.

Kelly Delaney stood there like an answer to a prayer.

"I'm sorry I'm late," she said. "I took a nap and fell asleep. I would have called but somebody was using the phone at the B and B."

She looked like a different woman than she had at the ice-cream shop. That woman had seemed exhausted, her face pale and her shirt so wrinkled it appeared as though she'd slept in it.

This woman wore slim-fitting blue capris and a darker blue short-sleeved shirt. She had thick, shining brown hair and a certain vitality in her face. He'd thought earlier she resembled Mandy, but now he saw her face possessed a sweetness that Mandy's lacked. Her hazel eyes were a little bigger and wider set, her brows thinner, her nose smaller with a tiny bump in the center.

He stepped back, playing it cool, trying not to let on how relieved he was to see her. "Come on in."

He went to shut the door behind her, noticing there

was no car in the driveway or at the curb. First no cell phone. Now no car? "Where's your car?" he asked.

"I walked," she said.

"From town?" Chase and his father lived outside the Indigo Springs city limits where houses were set back from a two-lane road on an acre of land or more.

"It wasn't far," she said.

It was a mile and a half, about a thirty-minute walk, most without the benefit of sidewalks. An easy distance for the hikers who regularly descended on Indigo Springs, but she wasn't wearing hiking shoes.

"Do you have a car?"

"Back home." She cleared her throat before she said, "I took the bus to Indigo Springs. It made more sense than driving, what with the wear and tear on my car and the high price of gas."

Yet she'd been able to afford a night in a bed-and-breakfast during the height of tourist season.

Toby let out a loud, baby laugh, drawing their attention. He'd balanced his torso on the ball, which rocked back and forth.

"That must be your son," Kelly said, an assumption Chase didn't correct. In all the ways that counted, he was Toby's father. She walked into the house, following the laugh as though Toby was a tiny Pied Piper. "He's precious! How old is he?"

"Twelve months," Chase said.

She clapped her hands and smiled at the baby. "You are such a cutie."

"Thank you," his father said.

Her head turned sharply, her eyes sparkling when

she spotted his dad. "I meant the baby, but you're not so bad, either."

His father still looked a little pale, but he laughed and extended his hand. "I'm Charlie Bradford, Chase's father."

"I'm Kelly," she said as they shook, then added almost as an afterthought, "Delaney."

"Nice to meet you, Kelly Delaney."

"What's your grandson's name?"

"Toby." His father didn't correct her misconception, either, but then he'd probably started thinking of himself as Toby's grandfather soon after Mandy moved in. Mandy had certainly treated him that way, leaving him alone with Toby for large chunks of time.

"Hi, Toby," she said brightly.

The baby turned at the sound of his name, gurgling out a greeting.

"You sure are a handsome devil, but that's not surprising." Kelly slanted his father a teasing look. "We've already established good looks run in the family."

His father beamed, his chest puffing out. Chase looked on in wonder. In the space of minutes, Kelly Delaney had managed to charm both his father and his baby. She might have captivated Chase, too, if he hadn't noticed how nervous she'd been at the ice-cream parlor. Something about her reactions had been off, something that warned him to beware.

"I hear you're going to help us find Mandy," his father announced. Obviously no internal warning system was cautioning him to beware. "Can you believe a mother could leave her baby the way she did, especially when Chase was so good to her? I told Chase she—"

"I haven't told Kelly about Mandy yet, Dad." Chase cut off his father in midsentence. "I wanted to show her the photos first."

"Of course," his father said, but he sounded puzzled.

Chase went to pick up the photographs he'd left on a side table while his father moved to cut off Toby, who was crawling toward the kitchen. Chase theorized the baby hadn't yet taken his first step because he was such a champion crawler.

"Oh, no, you don't." His father bent down, grimacing as though movement was difficult, then he swung the boy into the air. He wrinkled his nose. "No wonder he's so happy. I think his diaper's loaded."

"I can change him, Dad," Chase offered. Although he was reluctant to leave his father alone with Kelly, he was more disinclined to take advantage of his father.

"No, I'll do it," his father said. "It makes sense to give him his bath now. You two have things to talk about."

His father left the room. Was his gait a bit slower than normal? Toby grinned at them over Chase's father's shoulder. "Bye-bye," the baby called.

"Bye-bye." Kelly waved, then waited until the pair was out of sight before she said, "Your dad's wonderful with him. You're lucky to have him."

"He tells me that all the time," Chase said. "It wouldn't be so annoying if he wasn't right."

He expected her to smile but she seemed suddenly tense and he realized she was staring at the photos he held. He wondered why she cared so much about finding Mandy. Could it really be because of something as simple as returning a lost necklace?

"Here you go." He handed her the photos, watching her carefully as she examined them. There were two of them, both shot by a neighbor at a backyard cookout. In the first, he and Mandy sat beside each other at a picnic table, their bodies not touching. The second photo was of Mandy and Toby. Mandy wasn't smiling in that one, either.

"It's her. It's Amanda," she cried, the relief evident not only in her voice but in her posture. "Her hair color's different but it's definitely her. Look at the necklace she's wearing in this photo. It's different than the one I have, but it's a similar style."

"She has a thing for jewelry," Chase said. "The necklace you have was one of her favorites."

She lifted her head to gape at him. "You recognized the necklace?"

"Yes," he confirmed.

"I don't understand. Why show me the photos if you were sure Amanda and your wife are the same woman?"

"She's not my wife," he corrected. "And I showed you the photos so you could be sure, too. I don't want you to hold anything back when you tell me where you met her and what she said to you."

"Did she leave you?"

He wouldn't have stated it quite that way, but he wasn't about to confide the complicated nature of his relationship with Mandy, not when large parts of Kelly's story didn't track. But he had to tell her something to get her to open up.

"She left almost three weeks ago," he said. "Aside from a message on my cell phone saying she couldn't stand living here any longer, I haven't heard from her."

"Why would she leave Toby behind?"

"She didn't much like being a mother, either," he replied truthfully, but he'd said enough. It was his turn to ask the questions. "You said you met her at a coffee shop in upstate New York. Where exactly?"

She didn't answer immediately. "Schenectady."

"When was this?"

"Last Saturday," she said. "Like I told you, it was crowded. There was an empty seat at my table, and she asked if she could take it."

"What did you talk about?"

"Nothing important. She seemed...frazzled. Nervous. She made a remark about not liking Schenectady any more than Indigo Springs. I got the impression she was passing through town."

Passing through. It was the same expression Kelly had used to explain what she was doing in Indigo Springs, which brought them to the most far-fetched part of her story. It had nagged at Chase all afternoon, because it just didn't compute.

"That's quite a coincidence that you ended up in Indigo Springs a week later," he said. "How did you happen to be in Pennsylvania?"

Another hesitation. "I was visiting friends. In Scranton." The geography only made a vague sense, which she seemed to realize. "I decided to take a detour."

Chase mentally reviewed her story. She was hundreds of miles from home, showing around a sketch of a woman who was essentially a stranger to return a necklace that wasn't worth much more than a hundred dollars.

Although she'd answered all his questions, there had

been long pauses before some of her replies as though she was thinking about what to say.

Chase wasn't buying her story, but he couldn't think of a single reason for her to lie. Before the night was over, he intended to unravel the puzzle.

The heavy sound of footsteps interrupted his thoughts. His father stumbled into the family room, his face gray, clutching at his chest.

"I put Toby…in his crib," he said haltingly.

Chase forgot about Kelly Delaney and her lies and sprang to his feet. He crossed the room to his father's side, his own chest seizing with worry. "Dad? What's wrong?"

"I think…I'm having…a heart attack."

CHAPTER FOUR

CHASE HAD ALWAYS BEEN GOOD in a crisis, but his mind rebelled. This couldn't be happening to his father, who always seemed so hale and hearty. So invincible. Yet his father's eyes were shut in obvious pain, his hand covering his heart, his face contorted with fear.

The same way Chase's mother had looked before she died.

Chase's mind flashed back nine months to the visit he'd paid to his parents while he was training to be a conservation officer. His father had gone to the grocery store to pick up milk. His mother had seemed overly quiet as she and Chase watched a *Seinfeld* rerun. She'd complained of not feeling well, then collapsed in the armchair, the canned laughter on television an incongruous backdrop.

No! his mind screamed. He couldn't lose his father that way, too.

He should have seen the warning signs. Earlier today his father had dismissed his back pain as a by-product of too much yard work. He hadn't mentioned his chest, but his discomfort had been obvious. Why hadn't Chase put it together?

"I'll call 911 and get them to send an ambulance." Kelly's voice, full of authority.

"No!" Chase stopped her before she reached a phone. He'd summoned an ambulance during his mother's attack, and she'd died before the EMTs had reached the house. "There's no time. I can get him to a hospital quicker myself."

He put his arm around his staggering father to support him, trying to figure out how best to get him into his Jeep. He'd left the vehicle in the garage, the door to which was off the kitchen.

"Where are your car keys?" Kelly asked.

It took him a moment to retrieve the information from his scrambled brain. "Hanging from a hook on the side of the refrigerator."

She rushed toward the kitchen, calling over her shoulder. "Do you have any aspirin?"

Of course. Aspirin thinned the blood, lessening the size of blood clots. He should have thought of that.

"In the long, thin cabinet on the left."

Chase's father was breathing laboriously, leaning heavily on him as they continued walking toward the kitchen.

"Chest hurts," he choked out.

"Hang in there, Dad," Chase said, fighting rising panic.

But then Kelly was there, meeting them with a glass of water in one hand, a single aspirin in the other, ordering his father to chew instead of swallowing because she'd read somewhere that chewing got the aspirin into the blood stream faster.

She stood by while his father crunched the aspirin,

then guided the glass to his lips with a sure, steady hand. "Don't drink too much. Great. That's great."

She was on the move again, opening the door that led from the house to the garage, handing Chase his keys, flipping the switch that operated the automatic garage door, helping Chase situate his father in the Jeep.

Acting as if she was part of the family instead of a relative stranger.

Toby, he thought.

He couldn't leave Toby with a woman he'd just met. A woman he'd convinced himself not ten minutes ago was lying.

"I need to take Toby with me," he said.

"Don't worry about Toby," she said. "I'll stay here with him."

"But—"

"Listen to me," she interrupted in that same calm, authoritative voice. "You need to get your father to a hospital. I promise I'll take good care of your son."

Her eyes bored into his, clear and convincing. His father groaned, the sound causing pain to Chase's own heart.

"If it'll ease your mind, call a neighbor while you're on your way," she suggested. "But you need to go. Right now!"

She was right. It was vital to get a heart-attack victim to a hospital as quickly as possible. Doctors could administer drugs that broke up clots, stopping the heart attack in progress and limiting damage. Chase made a snap decision, the only one he could make.

"Okay, I'm going." He rushed around to the driver's side of the Jeep and got in.

His father was slumped in the seat, secured by the seat belt that Kelly had already fastened.

"Kelly's a good woman," his father muttered out the side of his mouth. "Toby'll be fine."

The fate of his father was less certain. His face was frighteningly pale. Chase turned the key in the ignition, mentally reviewing the winding route to the nearest hospital, figuring out how fast he dared drive to give doctors the best chance to save his father.

The trip passed in a blur, with Chase dividing his attention between the road and his father. It seemed an eternity before he pulled up to the emergency room.

Incredibly his father was able to walk into the hospital under his own power, with minimal help from Chase. The E.R. staff didn't take any chances when Chase reported his father was suffering from chest pain. The nurses hustled him into a wheelchair and transported him into an examining room.

Somebody asked Chase to move his pickup from the emergency-room entrance. When he returned to the waiting room, an admissions clerk summoned him to her cubicle and instructed him to fill out paperwork.

Only then did Chase have time to phone Judy Allen, the mother of three who lived a few doors down, to ask her to check on Toby and Kelly. He got a return call an hour later, shortly after the E.R. doctor informed him they were running tests on his father.

"Kelly has everything under control. She was putting Toby to sleep when I got here, and we're just sitting here talking," his neighbor told him. "How's your father?"

Chase didn't find out the answer for another hour, a

diagnosis his father was still marveling over much later as they drove home through the dark night, traveling at a much lower rate of speed.

"Heartburn," his father repeated. "Can you believe it was only heartburn?"

"Now that I know you had chili for lunch, yes," Chase said. "I should have asked what you'd had to eat, but the back pain threw me. That's a warning sign."

"In this case, it was only a sign that I'd been working in the yard," his father groused.

"Hindsight," Chase said, as he pulled the Jeep into the garage. "Don't beat yourself up over it."

The house was silent, the peace almost absolute, suggesting that no one was awake. Chase put a finger to his lips and peeked into the family room.

Kelly was asleep on the coach, one hand resting on a slightly flushed cheek, still wearing her tennis shoes. Judy was gone.

"She's asleep," he whispered to his father.

"This old fool needs to get some sleep, too," his father said. "But better an old fool than a dead fool."

His eyes moistening at the thought that his father could have met the same end as his mother, Chase impulsively embraced the other man. "Good night, Dad," he whispered.

"Good night, son." His father clapped him on the back, his voice as unsteady as Chase's.

After his father went upstairs, Chase quietly approached the sofa. Kelly's face looked even sweeter in sleep, her lashes sweeping her cheeks, her lips slightly parted as she breathed in and out softly.

He gently removed her shoes, then straightened. She stirred, rearranging herself into a more comfortable position. He held himself immobile, reluctant to make a sound that would wake her. He'd check on Toby next, but he already knew with a soul-deep certainty that the baby was fine.

The irony struck him even as he watched her sleep.

A few hours ago he didn't trust she'd told him the truth about Mandy, but he'd trusted her with something infinitely more precious.

Toby.

His desperation to find Mandy had driven his suspicion but his gut made the decision to accept what Kelly had told him at face value.

What possible reason could she have to lie anyway?

KELLY AWAKENED THURSDAY morning to the sounds of a baby's giggles, followed by a man's deep laughter.

Unlike the previous afternoon when she'd woken up disoriented after dreaming of Mandy and the kidnapped baby, she knew instantly where she was. She'd fallen asleep on the sofa while waiting for Chase Bradford and his father to return from the hospital.

She remembered her eyelids growing heavy while she puzzled over why a woman who left behind a baby as darling as Toby would resort to kidnapping. Thinking she'd rest for just a little while, she'd closed her eyes. Now it was morning.

"Here comes the train," she heard Chase say. "Choo choo choo choo. Open the tunnel."

She swung her legs off the sofa and got to her bare feet. Had someone taken off her shoes? She put them on, then found a bathroom where she smoothed her hair and clothes the best she could before following the voices to the kitchen.

"Good job, buddy." Chase sat in front of Toby's high chair, a small bowl of oatmeal in front of him.

Toby rapped his hands on the pull-down tray, his face and bib surprisingly free of food splatter. The choo-choo had a good engineer.

"Let's try an airplane. Scratch that. Too ordinary. How 'bout a flying saucer? Your mouth can be a black hole. Open up." Chase made believe the spoon was flying, then started humming the theme to *X-Files*.

Kelly laughed aloud.

Chase swung his head around, grinning when he spotted her watching them, yesterday's suspicion no-where in sight. He was already dressed in his ranger's uniform, the light-khaki color of the shirt bringing out the tan of his skin. Funny how she hadn't noticed what a handsome man he was until this moment.

"We've got company, bud. Could be the government. There could be trouble if she reports a UFO sighting." His spoon was still hovering above Toby's mouth. "Quick. Open up. Get rid of the evidence."

Toby might have been obeying Chase or he might have been smiling with his mouth open. Either way, Chase put the spoon in his mouth and the oatmeal—er, the UFO—disappeared.

"Way to go, Toby!" Chase raised his palm, parting

his middle and ring fingers in the Vulcan salute from the old *Star Trek* shows. Toby clapped with glee.

"Doesn't that mean live long and prosper?" Kelly asked.

"Not in this case," Chase said. "In this case it means Toby just kicked some baby butt. Didn't you, sport?"

The baby laughed louder, making it impossible not to join in. With Chase's face creased in a smile and laugh lines showing around his eyes, he barely resembled the man who'd questioned her with such fervor the night before. Her inability to understand Mandy deepened. The woman hadn't left only her baby, she'd left Chase.

"I hope you slept okay," he said.

"I did," she said, surprised it was true. Since her arrest, a good night's sleep had been an elusive commodity. "But you should have woken me when you got back."

"I tried," he said, "but you couldn't hear me over your snores."

Horrified, she put a hand to her mouth. "I'm sorry. I didn't know I snored."

"You don't," he said, laughing. "In fact, you hardly make a sound. But you should have seen your face when you thought you did."

Toby joined Chase's laughter, although he couldn't possibly have understood the trick Chase had played.

"You think that's funny, do you, Toby?" She ruffled the boy's blond head. "Don't tell anyone, but I do, too."

"Whew. That's a relief." Chase wiped a hand across

his brow. "I'd hate to insult the woman who did me such a huge favor."

"It was nothing," she said.

"It was most definitely something. You stayed with Toby so I could get my dad to the hospital."

"Your neighbor told me it was heartburn," she said. He'd phoned the house when the results of the EKG had come back, explaining that his father's heart had checked out fine.

"We didn't know that at the time," he said. "If it had been a heart attack, you might have saved his life. You were great. I panicked."

"You didn't panic."

"I did." He blew breath out his nose, his jaw clenching. After a few moments, he said, "My mom died of a heart attack not even a year ago. When I saw him standing there, clutching his chest… Well, all I could think was how much I didn't want to lose him."

Her own heart softened at the sorrow that laced his words. "I'm sorry about your mother, but you would have done fine even if I hadn't been here."

"Probably." He met her eyes. "But I'm glad you were here."

Toby cried out something incomprehensible, but made it understood he was less than pleased that he'd ceased to be the center of attention.

"Easy there, sport." Chase bent over and undid Toby's bib, smiling when the baby stroked his cheek. To Kelly, he said, "Could you watch him for a minute? I'll wake my dad, then drive you back to town on my way to work."

"Please, don't," she said, stopping him in his tracks. "Your father had a rough night. He could use more sleep. I'll stay with Toby until he wakes up."

He frowned, obviously reluctant to agree. Why shouldn't he be distrustful? Kelly asked herself. He clearly hadn't believed her story about the necklace. Despite what had happened last night, she was still a stranger.

"I'm sorry," she said. "I wasn't thinking. Of course you don't want to leave Toby with me."

"That's not—"

"I should apologize for sending your neighbor home last night," she interrupted. "But she was so tired she couldn't keep her eyes open, and she needs to get up early with her youngest. I didn't think you'd mind."

"I didn't," he said.

"Of course we're nearly strangers and…" She trailed off as his denial penetrated her brain. "Do you mean that? Were you really okay with me sending your neighbor home last night?"

"Yes," he said. "I'm okay with you staying with Toby now, too. I just don't want to take advantage of you."

"You wouldn't be," she refuted. "Really. I'd like to stay with him."

"Are you sure?"

"If you are."

He picked up his car keys, kissed Toby on top of the head and grinned at her. "Of course I'm sure. What did you think? That I'd be afraid you'd run off with him?"

"No," she managed to choke out, imagining how he'd react if he knew the charges she was facing. "Of course not."

"If you want, leave the necklace and I'll see Mandy gets it when I find her," he said. "I've gotta run. How 'bout you? Are you going back to New York today?"

"I, uh, haven't decided." She hadn't found out all she could about Mandy, but launching an interrogation when he'd apparently abandoned his didn't seem wise.

"Help yourself to coffee and whatever's in the refrigerator," he called.

He was halfway out of the kitchen before he hesitated, turned around and retraced his steps, not stopping until he stood directly in front of her. She tipped her chin, her gaze focusing on his mouth. His lips were lush, a tantalizing contrast to his masculine features. Her breath caught and for a crazy moment, she thought he was going to kiss her. But then he stuck out a hand.

She took it, and a bizarre sensation hit her like tiny fingers dancing over her skin.

"I'm sorry about all those questions last night," he said. "If I don't see you again, thanks. For everything."

He was dismissing her, she realized. He held on to her hand for a few moments longer. Or maybe she was the one doing the holding. Then he let go and she felt…bereft. And guilty as hell for convincing him she'd told the truth about Mandy.

When he was gone, she attached the suction toy she found on the kitchen table to Toby's high chair, taking in his oatmeal breath and the lingering smell of baby powder.

"What do you think, Toby?" she asked him while he played with the colorful toy's spinning, sliding, blinking shapes. "Am I a terrible person? And did you see me almost drool when he shook my hand? I mean, he's hot, but really."

"I don't think you're a terrible person because you think my son's hot." Charlie Bradford said, grinning at her from under the archway that led to the kitchen.

Kelly's face suddenly felt so warm it was as if she'd fallen asleep under a tanning lamp. "I didn't know you were there."

"You can find out the darnedest things by eavesdropping on people talking to themselves," he said, obviously unaware he'd misinterpreted at least one of her comments.

"Chase just left." She changed the subject, hoping he'd let what she'd said drop. "I offered to stay so you could sleep in."

"Thanks, but my alarm spoiled that plan." He walked over to Toby and stroked his blond head. "'Morning, buddy."

"How are you feeling this morning?" Kelly asked.

"Foolish." He went to a cupboard and pulled out two mugs. He held one up to her. "Coffee?"

"Please." She added that she liked it with cream but no sugar. "And don't feel foolish. I think it's a common mistake."

"That's what they told me in the E.R." He poured the coffee and added the cream. "But I still can't help feeling my son is a heartbreaker while I'm a heartburner."

So much for trying to change the subject.

"I'm too smart to get my heart broken by a man who's involved with someone else, Charlie."

"Chase isn't involved with anyone else," he denied.

"Not even the mother of his son?"

"Toby's not Chase's son."

"But the clerk at the B and B said…" Kelly's voice trailed off, trying to remember exactly what the friendly woman had said after Kelly asked for directions to Chase's house. "She said Mandy moved in with Chase when she got pregnant."

"She didn't mean pregnant with Toby." Charlie carried both coffee mugs to the kitchen table, then sat down beside her. Toby was happily occupied with the toy. "Chase and Mandy met earlier this year. She lived with us until her miscarriage."

Kelly shoved aside the momentary guilt that she was about to ply Chase's father for information about his son. "So he's not in love with her?"

"Never was. But you've got to understand something about my boy. He always tries to do the right thing. So when Mandy told him she was pregnant, he stepped up. I'm sure he would have asked her to marry him."

Kelly drank her coffee, thinking about Chase doing the honorable thing. She couldn't quite believe he didn't have feelings for Mandy.

"If he doesn't love her, why is he looking for her?"

"To get her to sign over custody of Toby," Charlie answered. "I'm praying she turns up soon because otherwise he's got this fool notion that he needs to go to DPW and do everything nice and legal. It seems his conscience gets heavier whenever anybody asks about Mandy."

"But you and Chase don't have any blood ties to Toby," Kelly said. "If you go to DPW, you could lose him."

"That's what I told him," Charlie said. "God knows he loves that boy, but I think the only thing stopping him from going to DPW is we can't be positive Mandy's not coming back. Not after three weeks."

"What has Chase done to try to find her?" she asked.

"Everything but poll the community, but that probably wouldn't help anyway," he said. "Mandy didn't socialize much. She didn't talk about out-of-town friends, she doesn't have any family Chase knows of and Smith is probably the most common surname in the United States. He didn't have a whole lot to go on until you showed up."

Guilt spiraled through Kelly for not revealing everything she knew, but she couldn't afford to trust anybody when a mistake could land her in prison. "I'm afraid I haven't been much help."

"I know. Chase told me about it last night. On the way back from the hospital," he added wryly, "not on the way there."

"Did she have any friends in town? Maybe they know something."

"She took a dislike to Indigo Springs right off the bat, so she didn't try very hard to fit in," Charlie said. "About the only effort she made was getting that waitress job."

Kelly's heart started to pound. If Mandy had held down a job, her employer would have records for tax purposes, maybe even references. If Kelly got names, she might find somebody who knew where Mandy was.

"Where was she a waitress?" she asked.

"Angelo's. Serves the best food in Indigo Springs, if you ask me," he said.

"Was that the only place she worked?"

"Only place I know of," he said, "although she did

apply for a job with the new lawyer in town. I remember because she was mad as a hornet when Sara didn't hire her."

"Mad?" Kelly thought that was strange. "Not disappointed?"

"Definitely mad. She went on and on about something or other. References, I think it was. Yeah, that's it. Something about her references."

Another avenue to explore if Kelly couldn't find the information she needed at the restaurant.

"Are you hungry?" Charlie asked. "I could get you some breakfast."

"No, thanks," she said, her mind already plotting ahead. If Angelo's was open for lunch, somebody should be at the restaurant as early as ten or eleven o'clock. "I'm staying at the Blue Stream B and B. Breakfast comes with the room."

Considering she hadn't used her room last night, she might as well get something for her money.

"Let me finish my coffee and I'll drive you back to town," he said.

"Oh, no. That's not necessary. It's such a beautiful morning, I can walk."

"A gentleman doesn't let a lady who spent the night on a sofa because of him walk back to her hotel," Charlie said. "Isn't that right, Toby?"

Toby looked up from his toy and grinned, then said something in a language only he could understand.

"See," Charlie said. "Toby says I'm absolutely right."

"In that case, how can I refuse?" Kelly said, but guilt laced her smile.

One Bradford male was just as charming as the next—and she was lying to all three of them. The fact that she didn't have a choice was small comfort.

A DRAWBACK TO LIVING IN a town known for its surrounding mountains was that there weren't many flat places to push a baby stroller.

Charlie Bradford and his late wife hadn't considered the terrain when they bought a vacation home in a hilly, tree-lined neighborhood. Neither had they looked for a place with sidewalks. But then Charlie hadn't anticipated ending up spending his retirement from the post office as a widower with primary care of a baby.

He didn't mind looking after Toby. He did mind that the only place relatively level enough to stroll him, weather permitting, was downtown Indigo Springs's sidewalks.

Especially because his lack of options had enabled one of the most beautiful women in town to find him.

"I hate that you didn't call me last night," Teresa Jessup said, keeping step beside him as he carefully navigated the stroller over a stretch of slightly uneven sidewalk.

At sixty-two, Teresa was five years younger than Charlie but could have passed for a decade younger than she was. Not that she tried. She had classic features, blond hair that made it difficult to see the gray and an aversion to cheating the aging process. Teresa was that much lovelier because she was completely natural.

"You know why I couldn't call you." Charlie lowered his voice to a whisper so Toby wouldn't hear, which he realized was silly. The baby had drifted off and wouldn't understand what was going on even if he was awake.

"So, if you had been having a heart attack and, God forbid, you'd died, I wouldn't know about it until I read your obituary in the newspaper?"

He usually loved the way her mind worked. She took a situation and zeroed in on what was most important, which was why she made such a good insurance agent. But in this case, she was exaggerating.

"Indigo Springs is still a pretty small town," Charlie said. "Somebody would have mentioned me dying before you saw it in the paper."

He couldn't be sure if she stamped her foot because they were, after all, walking. "You know what I mean, Charlie Bradford."

"I know you're making a big deal out of nothing," he said. "Have a little compassion, woman. Do you know how embarrassing it is to go to the emergency room for heartburn?"

"That's not the point."

"Although I've gotta tell you the doctor was pretty understanding," he continued as though she hadn't interrupted. "I had my heart checked out after Emily died, but he said you can never be too careful about these things."

"Are you all right?" She laid a hand on his arm, her blue gaze searching his face. He was reminded that six years ago her husband, Bill, had also died of a heart attack. "Is there something wrong with you that you're not telling me?"

"I scheduled a physical Monday just to be sure, but the E.R. doc said it was nothing that laying off spicy foods won't cure," he said. "But, you know, my blood pressure would be lower if you used that pretty mouth of yours to smile at me instead of arguing with me."

She smiled, just as he hoped, but it was a grudging smile. "I don't know why I put up with you, Charlie Bradford."

"Because I'm hands-down the sexiest man you've ever known," he suggested.

She laughed.

"I don't like the sound of that laugh. Who do you know sexier than me? Anybody under sixty doesn't count." He waggled his eyebrows at her.

"You make it really hard to stay mad at you," she said.

"Then don't stay mad," he suggested. "We're still on for tonight, right? Eight o'clock."

"Yes, we're still on," she said. "But don't think for a minute that we're not going to hash this out."

They had been walking in the area of town where pedestrian traffic was lightest, but now more people were on the sidewalk. Most of them were tourists paying attention to the businesses lining the street rather than to Charlie and Teresa, but he couldn't be too careful.

"We can hash it out when there aren't so many people around," he said in a soft voice.

She huffed out a breath, loud enough that he heard it. "I suppose you're not crazy about us walking through town together, either."

He didn't reply, because she knew very well his position on the subject.

"Fine," she said. "But one way or the other, we're settling this tonight."

He nodded, already trying to think of ways he could

distract her when tonight came. She picked up her pace, putting distance between herself and the baby stroller. The rigid set of her shoulders gave away her displeasure.

She looked like a woman who'd had enough.

A touch of what felt like last night's heartburn returned, making his chest hurt. This time the reason wasn't spicy food, but a sick feeling that she might have run out of patience.

Then, as she was waiting to cross a side street, she turned around.

The heavy feeling in his chest lessened. He grinned and waved, thinking that he just might be able to buy some more time after all.

CHAPTER FIVE

KELLY'S PALMS SWEATED and her stomach clutched as she waited for the owner of Angelo's to react to her story about the broken necklace. The more she told the tale, the more holes it seemed to have.

Or maybe, after apparently convincing Chase she was telling the truth, she'd lost her taste for lying.

Kelly shored up her nerve and looked Aaron Hirschell directly in the eyes, reminding herself she'd do whatever it took to find Mandy.

Hirschell cast a backward glance at the kitchen, one of many since he'd reluctantly responded to her loud knocking. He'd already told her the restaurant wouldn't be open for business for another thirty minutes.

"Mandy doesn't work here anymore so I don't understand why you came to me." Hirschell tapped his foot against the glazed porcelain-tile floor. He was a fair-skinned, light-haired man in his fifties, as far removed from Kelly's image of an Italian restaurant owner as he could be.

Kelly relaxed slightly, relieved he hadn't asked any questions about the necklace. "I thought you might be able to tell me about her. Previous address. Names of references. Any information that would help me find her."

"Find her? What happened to her? Is she a missing person?"

Kelly stifled a groan. She was loathe to make trouble for Chase by advertising that Mandy had abandoned her child.

"Oh, no, nothing like that," Kelly insisted. "She's out of town, that's all."

The interested light left his eyes. "If she's out of town, ask that forest ranger she lives with where she is. A good guy. Name of Chase Bradford. He's probably in the phone book."

Kelly hesitated, mentally phrasing her response so he wouldn't know she'd been in contact with Chase. "Since I'm already here, I might as well find out what you know."

His arms crisscrossed over his chest, his foot tapping a steady beat, his brows drawing together. "Not much. She only worked here a few weeks."

"Then you must still have her application," Kelly said, then added lightly, "and her employment papers."

Specifically her tax form. If Kelly could get her hands on Mandy's social security number...

"What business is that of yours?" Hirschell's demeanor switched at a lightning clip from impatience to suspicion. "Are you some kind of investigator?"

Kelly could have kicked herself. In her zeal to find Mandy, she'd gone too far. "Of course not. Why would you think that?"

"You come in here, telling some cock-and-bull story about a necklace, then wonder how I caught on to you."

He pointed his index finger toward the door. "I'd like you to leave."

"But—"

"Just go." He waved her away with a sweep of his hand, pivoted on his heel and disappeared into the kitchen.

She stared after him, trying to figure out why he thought she was a private investigator, and why he'd gotten so upset. Asking about Mandy's employment papers admittedly was a mistake since they were confidential, but it shouldn't have put him on the defensive unless...

He suspected Kelly not of being a private eye but of investigating tax fraud for the IRS. It could be that Aaron Hirschell was paying his waitresses under the table.

The theory crystallized during her next stop, the law office of Sara Brenneman.

The lawyer was a tall, engaging brunette dressed in a leopard-skin top and slacks instead of a business suit. She sported a sparkly engagement ring Kelly might not have noticed if Sara hadn't kept fingering it.

"You're going to all this trouble because of a necklace?" Sara quirked a brow, her demeanor even more skeptical than the restaurant owner's. Kelly didn't dare wipe her damp palms on her blue-jean skirt.

"The necklace is a favorite of hers." Kelly didn't know if that was true, but it could be. "She'd want it back."

"Then why not leave the necklace with Chase Bradford?"

Kelly repeated the name as though she'd never heard it before. "Chase Bradford?"

"He's a really good guy," Sara said, marking the third

time today somebody had vouched for Chase's character. First Chase's father, then the restaurant owner and now Sara. "I'm sure he'd help you. He and Mandy were living together until she left town."

Kelly noted that Sara used the past tense. She warned herself to tread carefully because her guess was that Sara and Chase were friends.

"I could get Chase on the phone for you," Sara offered, bolstering Kelly's theory.

"Thank you but I'd really like to hear what you know about Mandy," Kelly said.

Sara had opted to sit in a chair beside Kelly rather than behind her desk. She angled her body and leaned forward at the waist, balancing her elbows on her thighs.

"Why come to me?" Sara sounded as though she was cross-examining a witness. "How can I possibly help you find Mandy?"

Kelly fought to keep her cool. "I heard Mandy interviewed with you for a job."

"That's true," she said slowly. "But who—?"

"I also heard Mandy was upset you didn't hire her, that it had something to do with her references. I thought you still might have them."

"Her references, you mean?" Sara asked, successfully sidetracked.

"Yes." Kelly nodded for emphasis. "I thought someone she used as a reference might know where she is."

"She was of the opinion she shouldn't have to give me any." Sara sounded bewildered by the assumption. "She made quite a scene about it, in fact."

Kelly's brain raced, speculating about what might have

happened next. Could Mandy have turned to an employer who didn't ask questions? Or, in Aaron Hirschell's case, possibly require any documentation at all?

Once Kelly made the intuitive leap, another theory took hold. No, not a theory, a conclusion.

Mandy was on the run from something. Maybe Mandy Smith wasn't even her real name, the way Kelly Delaney wasn't hers.

It takes one to know one, she thought.

"Do you know if she was friends with anybody in town?" Kelly asked. "Or anywhere she used to hang out?"

"I saw her a couple times at the Blue Haven."

Kelly recognized the name as belonging to a pub on Main Street.

"But let's backtrack," Sara said. "Who told you Mandy applied for a job with me?"

Kelly shifted in her seat, concluding she had no choice but to tell the truth. Sara would surely figure out if she lied. "Charlie Bradford."

"Charlie?" Sara looked shocked. "If you know Charlie, why haven't you talked to Chase?"

"Chase doesn't know where she is." Before Sara could point out that Kelly had given the impression she'd never heard of Chase, Kelly stood up. "Thanks for your time. I won't take up any more of it."

Kelly squelched an urge to sprint for the exit, proceeding as though panic wasn't squeezing her lungs. She didn't take a deep breath until she was across the street from the law office in the sunshine of a lovely summer afternoon.

She wasn't cut out for a life on the run, she thought as she composed herself. If she didn't show up for her preliminary hearing next Friday, however, a bench warrant would be issued for her arrest.

She headed for the Blue Haven with purpose in her step, praying that Mandy had confided her plans to somebody who worked there and wishing she wasn't so alone.

She wished she could confide in Chase Bradford, who had a compelling reason of his own to find Mandy.

But even though Chase's father, the restaurant owner and the lawyer had vouched for him, Kelly couldn't afford to trust anybody with her freedom.

CHASE DISCONNECTED THE cell-phone call, swung his Jeep from the two-lane road into the gravel parking lot adjacent to a trailhead, turned around and headed back toward Indigo Springs.

He'd planned to spend the rest of today patrolling his territory for illegal hunting and fishing activity, but that would have to wait.

Kelly Delaney was reportedly questioning people in Indigo Springs who knew Mandy, which spelled trouble. Plenty of people were aware Mandy had left town, but precious few realized Chase had no idea where she'd gone. Once word spread that her whereabouts were unknown, he'd no longer be able to justify withholding news of Toby's abandonment to DPW.

He could hardly defend his actions now, even though dread filled him at the prospect of losing Toby and his father kept insisting it was too soon to alert the authorities.

This morning when he'd said goodbye to Kelly, he'd given up hope she had any information that could help him find Mandy. After a phone call from Sara Brenneman, who'd recently become engaged to Chase's friend Michael Donahue, he wasn't so sure.

"Something's not right with her," Sara told him after reporting Kelly had paid her a visit. "Why would she go to such lengths to return a necklace?"

That question had raised Chase's initial suspicions, which he'd let fade when Kelly took over during his father's crisis. She'd been clearheaded, caring and competent, the perfect antidote to Chase's panic.

He'd discovered something else about Kelly the morning after the wild ride to the hospital emergency room—he enjoyed being around her. She had an understated sense of humor that he found attractive and a nurturing quality that Mandy lacked.

She'd proven he could trust her with Toby, so he'd allowed himself to believe she was who she said she was: A woman doing a good deed after a chance encounter with Mandy.

Sara's phone call had resurrected his doubts—and his questions. For the life of him, Chase still couldn't come up with a reason for Kelly to lie.

After he found a coveted parking spot on Main Street, he placed a quick call to one of his buddies in the police department, asking him to find out what he could about a Kelly Delaney from Schenectady, New York.

Then he went in search of Kelly. He found her on a bar stool at the Blue Haven Pub, which Sara had tipped him off as her destination. She looked like an all-American girl in a blue-jean skirt and gauzy yellow top, her thick brown hair loose around her shoulders. She was chatting with Annie Sublinski, who ran an outfit down by the river that offered whitewater, biking and hiking excursions.

The booths and tables were filling up, a sign that the owners of the pub had made a good decision to open the bar for lunch during tourist season. Only Kelly, Annie and two men holding a loud, not entirely friendly conversation had opted to sit at the bar. The men looked to be in their twenties with identical shaved heads. The thinner of the two sported a goatee while his buddy had a chin-strap beard.

Chase slipped onto the stool next to the women. "Hi, ladies."

"Hi, Chase," Annie said easily.

Kelly shifted her attention from Annie, her mouth and eyes rounding. Was that guilt he glimpsed in her expression?

"Chase," she said. "I thought you were working."

"Just taking a short break." He looked around her to Annie. "How about you, Annie? Isn't this high season? How can you tear yourself away from business in the middle of the afternoon?"

"Desperation. I'm short guides this weekend so stopped by to rope Jill into doing a run for me." She nodded to the bartender, a young woman with short, curly black hair who was delivering another round of drinks to the two men at the opposite end of the bar. "I've been short-handed since Kenny Grieb went back to being an auto mechanic."

"Annie's so desperate she even asked if I was the outdoors type," Kelly supplied.

"You never know when you're going to find another—" Annie stopped talking in midsentence, her face growing pale, her hand rising to cover the birthmark on one side of her face. Her gaze focused on a spot behind Chase. He turned to see Ryan Whitmore, the doctor who'd given him his physical last week, walk into the bar. An older man waved Ryan over to the booth farthest from where they sat.

"Do you know that man, Annie?" Kelly asked.

"Used to," Annie said, her voice oddly strangled. "He must be visiting."

"He's doing more than visiting," Chase said. "He's filling in for his sister. She broke her leg so he'll be here at least two months, maybe more."

"Two months," Annie repeated, her lips moving but hardly any sound escaping. She got up abruptly from the bar stool, mumbling something about getting back to work before she hurried out the front door.

"That was odd," Kelly remarked at the same time the man with the goatee loudly accused his drinking companion of moving in on his girlfriend.

Jill the bartender was heading their way, but cast a wary glance backward as one man told the other he was imagining things.

"What can I get you?" Jill asked Chase. It was too early for lunch so he ordered a soda. While Jill poured his drink, he checked on the two men he'd mentally started referring to as Goatee and Chin Strap. Goatee seemed mollified by Chin Strap's denial, but Chase sensed trouble ahead.

Jill pushed the soda toward him. "Seems like I've seen you in here before."

"A few times." Chase hadn't had much opportunity to hang out in bars since Toby had entered his life, something that hadn't stopped Mandy even though at the time she'd been pretending to be pregnant. "I would have been with a redhead. Mandy Smith."

"We were just talking about her," Jill exclaimed as though it was a coincidence. "Mandy used to come in here pretty regularly and sit at the bar, but I haven't seen her in a couple of weeks."

Chase waited for Kelly to ask why a pregnant woman had hung out in a bar, but she didn't. Hell, maybe she thought Mandy had been drinking tonic water.

"Jill was just telling me how she and Mandy used to talk about vintage costume jewelry," Kelly supplied.

"We like the same kind of thing." The bartender gestured to her necklace. A large round silver pendant set with black onyx dangled from a silver chain interlocked with black onyx stones. Chase would have been hard-pressed to tell it was a reproduction.

"Did Mandy ever talk about other things, like her out-of-town friends or places she wanted to visit?" Chase asked.

"Not that I can remember. Aside from the jewelry, she mostly talked about how much she hated Indigo Springs." Jill tipped her head. "Why do you want to know? Did something happen to her?"

"Nothing like that," Chase interjected, wondering how long it would be before it spread through town Mandy was gone. "She left word that she needed to get away for a while. She just didn't say where she was going."

Jill waved a hand. "I wouldn't worry. Mandy always

seemed wound up pretty tight so she probably just wanted some space. She'll come back in her own time."

"Yeah," Chase said, although it seemed increasingly likely that Mandy truly had abandoned her son.

"So you really have no idea where she might have gone?" Kelly sounded as desperate for a clue as Chase, causing him another prick of suspicion. "I'm really eager to get the necklace back to her."

"It must be some necklace," Jill commented, telling Chase he wasn't off base. Kelly's story didn't hold weight. "Can I see it?"

"Sure," Kelly said, fishing the necklace from her purse.

A movement at the end of the bar drew his eye. A thin, short woman with straight, coal-black hair had joined the two men. She directed Goatee to move over a bar stool and sat down between him and Chin Strap.

"I remember Mandy wearing this!" Jill exclaimed.

The bartender held the ends of Mandy's necklace in either hand. The afternoon sun streamed through an overhead window and struck the fake jewels, making them glint.

"This necklace was one of her favorites," Jill continued. "I think it's a Heffinger."

Kelly frowned. "A what?"

Jill laughed. "It's a who. Helene Heffinger. She's a very talented jewelry designer. She usually signs her pieces." She turned over the broken clasp and read the signature. "I was right. It is a Heffinger."

"This Heffinger, does she have a shop somewhere?" Chase asked, already thinking about sales receipts and records.

"Nope. Doesn't have the temperament for it. You can't find her on the Internet, either. She's old-school, kind of a tough old broad."

"Then how do her customers find her?" The question came from Kelly, whose forearms rested on the bar as she leaned forward.

"She's a regular on the craft-show circuit. Come to think of it, there's a show down in Allentown this weekend. She lives somewhere in the Lehigh Valley so I'm betting she'll be there."

"Hey, barkeep!" Chin Strap yelled, his words slurring. "Can we get a beer for the lady?"

"Be right there," Jill called, then handed the necklace back to Kelly.

Silence stretched a few beats after the bartender left until Chase broke it. "You're thinking of going to that craft show."

"I *am* going. Helene Heffinger might keep a mailing list of her customers. She might have a phone number or an old address for Mandy." Kelly voiced the possibilities that had run through Chase's head. "You're going, too, aren't you?"

"Yeah," he said, "but my going makes sense. I've got Mandy's baby. You've got her necklace. A necklace I said I'd return for you."

She moistened her lips. "How can you return it when you don't know where Mandy is, either?"

The verbal dancing had gone on long enough. He pinned her with his gaze. "Why is it so important for you to find her?"

"I already told you," she said. "To give her back the necklace."

She looked him straight in the eyes, the way somebody who was telling the truth would, but he wasn't falling for her act anymore. Too much didn't make sense, including the sketch she'd drawn of Mandy. Who went to that much trouble to return a relatively inexpensive piece of jewelry to a stranger?

"You're lying," he said.

She flinched, alerting him that his barb had hit the mark. She pressed her lips together and dropped her gaze. He waited for the inevitable denial, but she surprised him.

"You're right," she said. "I am lying."

KELLY WAS GOING TO tell Chase about everything. The kidnapped baby. Agreeing to babysit for Mandy. The arrest. Skipping out on bail. Everything.

It wasn't surprising that he'd accused her of being untruthful. In fact, she'd been waiting for the charge. After enduring round after round of interrogation with the Wenona cops, she recognized when somebody didn't believe her.

She'd gotten a reprieve last night when his father had stumbled into the room clutching his chest, but now was her time of reckoning. She had no choice but to trust him.

"The reason I'm looking for Mandy has nothing to do with that necklace," she said.

A clattering at the opposite end of the bar interrupted her. The man with the scraggly beard, the one accused of moving in on his friend's girl, lay sprawled on the floor beside an overturned bar stool.

The man with the goatee stood over him, shouting, "I told you not to touch her!"

"It was just a little kiss! It didn't mean anything." The petite woman pushed at her boyfriend's chest, but he didn't budge.

"You shouldn't have got me mad." The man on the floor rose unsteadily to his feet, lending credence to his statement. He was about five inches taller and forty pounds heavier than his friend. He raised his fists, boxer-style.

"Somebody should call the police," Kelly said.

"No need. I got it." Chase left his bar stool and strode toward the men.

"What do you mean you got it? It's a bar fight!" Kelly called after him, but he didn't turn back.

She watched in horror as the gap between Chase and the two men narrowed. The bigger man cocked his right fist, looking able to mow down everything in his past. First his buddy with the goatee, then Chase. Just as the big man was about to let his fist fly, Chase pounced. He intercepted the big man and twisted his right arm behind his back.

"Ow," the big man cried. "That hurts."

The man with the goatee took a step forward, as though he meant to smack the other man while he was effectively immobilized.

"Do it and you'll spend the night in jail," Chase told him in a gruff voice. He looked tough and in control, a startling contrast to the gentle man who'd pretended his oatmeal-filled spoon was a UFO that morning.

The man with the goatee retreated, his palms raised in surrender. "We don't want no trouble. Right, Frankie?"

"Right," Frankie parroted in a pain-filled, high-pitched voice, his arm still pinned behind his back. "No trouble."

"Then get out of here and get some black coffee into you." Chase released Frankie, who stumbled backward, rubbing his arm. "Any more trouble from either of you, and I'll arrest you for being drunk and disorderly."

"No. No. We're going." The instigator turned into the peacemaker. He took some bills from his wallet and threw them on the bar before grabbing his girlfriend's hand and slinging an arm around his buddy's shoulder. He set a quick pace to the exit.

Chase returned to his seat, looking as though the miracle he'd just accomplished was all in a day's work.

"That was impressive," Kelly said. "You really had them believing you could arrest them."

"I *can* arrest them."

She thought over their first meeting when he'd confirmed he wasn't a cop. His badge still said he worked for the Department of Fish and Wildlife. "I thought you were a forest ranger."

"I'm also a law-enforcement officer," he said. "I deal mostly with fish and wildlife regulations, but if I see the law being broken, it's my job to enforce it."

Violating her bail after being arrested for kidnapping would constitute breaking the law.

Kelly's heart pounded so hard if felt as though her rib cage might splinter. Her first impression had been correct. Chase Bradford was a danger to her. If he discovered she was in violation of her bail, he'd be duty bound to turn her in. She felt sick when she thought about how close she'd come to sealing her own fate.

But maybe she was overreacting. She was an innocent woman and by all accounts Chase was a decent man. She could possibly convince him she'd been wrongly accused and enlist his help in clearing her name. She just had to summon the courage to tell him and pray he wouldn't go by the book.

He always tries to do the right thing.

Charlie Bradford's words about his son resonated in her mind even as she thought about confessing. Could she really take the chance that Chase's interpretation of the "right course of action" would coincide with hers?

"Getting back to what we were talking about," Chase said, "you were about to tell me why you're really looking for Mandy."

She couldn't tell him the truth. The realization hit her with enough force that she recoiled. The stakes were far too high to gamble away her freedom.

"Well?" he prodded. "Why are you looking for her?"

"She stole money from me." Kelly forced herself not to squirm. Neither did she drop her gaze nor let guilt over her dishonesty creep into her consciousness. This was about survival. She couldn't let him suspect she was about to tell another lie.

"I thought you met her at a coffee shop."

"I did." Kelly paused, trying to remember what she'd told him previously. "And she did ask if she could sit at my table. It wasn't until later that I discovered it was because she planned to empty my bank account."

"I don't understand," he said.

"I didn't, either. At first. But she must have been

standing behind me in line and saw my password when I used my debit card."

He was quiet, waiting for her to continue. Now that she knew he was in law enforcement, his silence reminded her of the tactic one of the Wenona cops had used. Instead of peppering her with questions, he'd said nothing, waiting for her to grow uncomfortable and blurt out something incriminating.

"My purse was on the chair between us," she said. "Mandy must have slipped the debit card out of my wallet when I went back to get extra napkins. That's the only thing I can figure."

He still said nothing, but Kelly wasn't about to offer any more information unless he asked for it. She'd come up with the story on the fly, figuring that money was always a good motivator, and was mentally reviewing it for loopholes.

He finally broke the silence. "Isn't there a limit to how much money you can withdraw from an ATM?"

"She made two withdrawals and only the first one was at an ATM. She must have gone inside a bank and found a teller who didn't ask questions because she just about cleaned me out."

He narrowed his eyes and shook his head, but she held his gaze, refusing to look away.

"Why didn't you go to the police?" he asked.

Of course. She should have anticipated that question.

"I called the police," she said. "But the cop I got on the phone didn't give me much hope I'd get my money back. Especially because it was pretty clear Mandy wasn't a local. That's why I decided to look for her myself. All the ATMs have cameras, so if I can find her I can prove she stole my card."

"Then why make up the story about the necklace?"

"I didn't make it up," she said. "She really did lose the necklace."

"You know what I mean. Why not just say you were looking for her because she stole from you?"

She made herself laugh, hoping she'd injected the right amount of disbelief. "I'm a stranger in town. I didn't know how people would react if I accused one of their own of stealing."

"But why not tell me?"

"You lived with her. You're the last one I'd tell." She took a deep breath. "Besides, you didn't tell me why you were looking for her, either. I had to find out from your father it's because you want custody of Toby."

"My father talks too much," he said. "But it's not the same thing. You lied to me. I failed to tell you something you didn't need to know."

"If we're going to be a team, it is something I need to know." The words were out of her mouth before she considered their wisdom. Did she really want to join forces with a man who had the power to arrest her?

His brows drew together. "What do you mean, 'a team'?"

"I'm not sure either of us can find Mandy on our own. Together, we have a pretty good shot," she said, thinking aloud. Yes, no matter the danger, she needed his help. She swallowed, then went for broke. "So how about it? Want to go to that craft show?"

Her story sounded credible, much better than the

last tale she'd invented, but she couldn't be sure he believed it.

She desperately needed him to believe her.

Finally, when she thought she couldn't stand the suspense any longer, he spoke. "I have to work tomorrow but I should be able to get away for a few hours in the morning."

Her limbs sagged with relief, but she strived to remain cool and collected. "Good."

"Just one more question," he said, and she tensed up again. "Do you really expect to get your money back if we find her?"

"I've come this far," she said. "I can only hope for the best."

CHAPTER SIX

THE RESTAURANT CHARLIE BRADFORD chose for his dinner with Teresa Jessup Thursday night was in a rustic inn an hour's drive from Indigo Springs. Over many years' worth of fishing trips, Charlie had passed the driveway that led to the lodge a half dozen times before he got curious enough to explore it.

Set a mile back from the main road in a copse of trees, the inn was charming, romantic and isolated. The restaurant just off the main lobby, with flickering candlelight gracing its tables, boasted the same qualities.

The place was so out of the way it seemed extremely unlikely Charlie would run into anyone who knew him, which was precisely the reason he'd chosen it. An added bonus was the proximity of an old buddy's fishing cabin, where Charlie had truthfully told Chase he was spending the night.

Charlie looked at his watch to confirm Teresa was indeed twenty minutes late, then took a swig of water and crunched a melting ice cube. The restaurant wouldn't be so perfect if he had to eat alone. He waited another ten minutes until it seemed likely that would be the case, but still told the waiter he wasn't yet ready to order.

Five minutes after that, Teresa finally came into the restaurant. Dressed in dark-cream slacks and a tan blouse that looked good with her blond hair, she made the entire restaurant seem brighter.

As always when he saw her, his heart flipped over. This time it tumbled a little more vigorously because he'd convinced himself she wasn't going to show.

"Hi, Terri," he said, feeling his lips curve upward.

"Don't you 'Hi, Terri' me." Her grumble would have worried him more if she'd sat across from him at the table for four instead of next to him, where their knees almost touched. He moved his knee so it would make contact with hers, encouraged when she didn't pull away. "I got stuck in a line of cars behind a tow truck and it took me an hour and twenty minutes to get here."

"I told you it was an hour's drive."

"If we'd gone to a restaurant in Indigo Springs, it would hardly have taken any time at all."

"Yeah, but everybody knows that good things come to those who drive a long way to get it." He winked at her.

A corner of her mouth quirked.

"If you want me. Here I am. Drive and get me," he said, butchering the lyrics of a once-popular song.

The opposite corner of her mouth lifted, creating the smile that could make him sink to his knees. Before the night was over, he might find himself there, begging for understanding.

"I swear," she said, "I don't know how you do that."

"Do what?"

"Make me forget why I'm mad at you."

"Who can stay mad at a charming devil like me?" He

reached for her hand and brought it to his lips. "I'd think it'd be nearly impossible."

Over the next hour while they dined on some of the best filet mignon he'd ever eaten, Charlie did his charming best to assure she didn't remember why she'd been annoyed at him. He told her about Kelly, entertained her with stories about Toby and listened to her talk about her shortened workweek.

"We'll pass on dessert and take the check," he told the waiter after consulting with Teresa. He waited until the young man was out of earshot, then leaned close to her, enjoying the subtle scent of her perfume. "Although it might be a good idea to cap off the meal."

Her brows drew together. "With what?"

"I'll give you a choice," he said. "Coffee, tea or me."

"Why, Charlie Bradford." She put a hand to her chest. "Are you asking me to spend the night with you?"

He'd lined up his friend's cabin for tonight and Friday precisely so he and Teresa could have privacy. Her office was closed tomorrow for the Fourth of July holiday weekend, leading him to tell Chase optimistically that he wouldn't be back until Saturday for the festival. But until this moment, he hadn't known he'd go through with asking Teresa to share his bed. Up to this point, they hadn't moved past a few unforgettable kisses.

"Yes," he said, all levity gone from his voice. "My friend's cabin is only a few miles from here and I've got the keys. So what do you say?"

"Yes to spending the night with you," she said decisively. "No to the cabin."

"It's a very nice cabin," Charlie said over the pounding

of his heart. Had he miscalculated? He would have sworn she wasn't the kind of woman who'd prefer a room at an inn. "You'll like it. Maybe not as much as you'll like me, but you won't be disappointed."

"That's not it, Charlie." She looked him straight in the eyes. "I'd rather we drive back to town and stay at my place."

Charlie ran a hand over his jaw, seeing how he'd walked right into that one. "You know we can't do that, Teresa."

"I don't know anything of the sort," she retorted with spirit. "I never should have agreed to meet you here. All this sneaking around makes it seem like you're ashamed of me."

He sighed, for once not able to think up a quick comeback. He'd been trying to avoid this conversation, but saw now it was inevitable. "I'm not ashamed of you, Teresa, but it's only been nine months since Emily died."

"That's just it, Charlie." She grabbed his hand and looked into his eyes, hers burning with purpose. "Emily's dead. She's not coming back. I'm sorry to be blunt, but she'd want you to move on."

"She wouldn't want people gossiping about her husband."

"Not when she was alive, she wouldn't," Teresa said. "But she's gone, Charlie. I don't see how us being together hurts her."

Charlie shook his head, wishing he had the words to make her understand. "It's too soon."

"A few minutes ago, you were ready to go to bed with me. It wasn't too soon then."

"I meant it's too soon to go public," he clarified.

"Where is this coming from, Charlie? Why do you care so much what people think?"

He found it too difficult to look into her eyes as he thought about how to answer. The hostess was greeting a middle-aged couple with a smile and some menus. Recognition shimmied through him. It was Marie and Frank Dombrowski, who often sat near him at Sunday services.

"Don't turn around. The Dombrowskis just walked into the restaurant." His lungs filled with air as he waited to see where the hostess would seat them. He muttered almost under his breath, "And I was so careful to pick a place where we wouldn't run into anybody we knew."

The hostess said something to the Dombrowskis, then pivoted, leading them to a table on the opposite side of the restaurant. Charlie sighed in relief. "I don't think they saw us but we should get out of here before they do."

"You're unbelievable," Teresa snapped. "I'm telling you I don't want to sneak around anymore and you're planning the great escape."

Color infused her face and her lips thinned. Charlie had never seen her so angry. "There's no one I'd rather be on the run with than you, Terri," he quipped.

"That Bradford charm of yours won't work this time, Charlie." She pushed her chair back from the table and stood. "Give me a call when you're ready to come out of the shadows."

She stalked away from him for the second time that day, but this time she didn't turn around and look back.

The meal he'd just eaten roiled in his stomach. He hadn't explained himself very well, but that shouldn't have been necessary. Teresa, of all people, should understand he was only afraid of the gossip reaching one particular person.

But then Teresa didn't know the intricacies of his straight-and-narrow son's personality quite as well as Charlie did.

Quite simply Charlie couldn't risk losing his son so soon after losing his wife.

He could almost guarantee Chase would never forgive either of them if he discovered his father was involved with his mother's best friend.

CHASE SET TOBY'S CARRIER on Teresa Jessup's kitchen table and rolled his shoulders, feeling weary even though it wasn't yet nine on Friday morning.

At dawn Toby's loud, happy babbling had pulled him out of a deep sleep. He'd struggled to get himself and the baby ready for the day, discovering it took a lot longer to breakfast, shower and dress without his father around.

It had taken even more time to line up an alternative babysitter after Judy Allen had cancelled, pleading a sick kid. The next nearest neighbor, who had offered to watch Toby anytime, wasn't home.

Chase briefly considered asking his father to cut his fishing trip short before he remembered the area around the cabin had no cell-phone reception.

Teresa had been all that stood in the way of having to take Toby along on the trip to Allentown.

"Thanks, Aunt Teresa." Chase wasn't sure when he'd started calling her Aunt Teresa; he only knew it felt right. His mother, after all, had once told him Teresa was the sister she never had. "You're sure he won't be too much trouble?"

"Of course he won't. I'm just glad my boss gave us a three-day weekend so I can help you out." Teresa sounded sincere but looked as if he'd rousted her from bed. Her feet were bare and she wore pink pajamas dotted with tiny white hearts. "Will you be gone all day?"

"Afraid so. I'm working this afternoon and evening but this morning we're headed to a craft show. We have a lead on Mandy. It might not pan out, but it's worth a shot."

"We?"

"I'm going with a woman who showed up in town looking for Mandy."

"Oh, yes. Your father told me about her," she said, the revelation a bit of a surprise. His father must be in more frequent contact with Teresa than he thought.

"It's unbelievable you still haven't heard from Mandy." Teresa's jaw tightened. She sounded as though she might start waving a finger at any moment. "Once you find her, you bring her to me. I'll see to it that she signs those custody papers."

It felt good to have her on his side. "I just might do that."

She unbuckled Toby from the carrier and lifted him into her arms. He grinned sleepily at her before shutting his eyes. Figures. Toby had worn out Chase and Toby was the one taking a nap. She smoothed the little boy's hair back from his forehead, causing it to stick up in tufts.

"Speaking of my dad," Chase said, "can I ask you something?"

She nodded but there was nothing nonchalant about

the gesture. The faint rumblings Chase had been getting that all wasn't right with his father grew louder.

"Have you noticed how strange he's been acting?" he asked.

He could swear her entire body tensed.

"What do you mean?" she asked.

"He's been coming home late and half the time I don't know where he's been. I don't even know if he went on this fishing trip with one of his buddies or if he's alone. Did he tell you anything?"

She pursed her lips and shook her head. "You know your father. It's hard to have a serious conversation with him."

"Yeah," Chase said. When his father didn't want to talk about something, he turned it into a joke. He'd been joking a lot lately. "It's worse now with Mom gone. I know how much he misses her."

"We all miss her," Teresa said.

"Not like he does," Chase said. "Come to think of it, that's probably it."

"What is?"

"Why he keeps going off by himself." He shook his head. "I don't know why I didn't put it together before. They were married for forty years. He's not going to forget about her in nine months. Hell, I wouldn't want him to."

She said nothing, not that he expected her to. He kissed her on the forehead, then planted a second kiss on the sleeping baby boy's head.

"With it being the Fourth of July weekend, I might not get off work until really late tonight," he warned.

"If you need me to keep Toby overnight, just let me

know," she said. "I have a crib set up in the guest room
for my grandchildren."

"You're the best," he told her. "My mom sure had
good taste in friends."

"And don't you forget it," she quipped, her eyes twin-
kling, the remark reminding him of his father.

He was smiling when he left the house, the memory
of his mother burning brighter, as it always did after he
spent time with Teresa.

He pulled his Jeep to the curb in front of the B and
B a short time later, wondering whether his mother
would have liked Kelly. Probably. His mom had always
advocated giving another person the benefit of doubt.

In Kelly's case, he was still trying to figure out if
that was wise.

She'd duped him once with the story about the necklace. Her assertion that Mandy had stolen from her was
more credible but still problematic. It was rare for a victim of a crime to hunt for the perpetrator and rarer still
for the victim to chase the criminal across state lines.

Caution had spurred him to get the check run on her
name. His friend in the police department had called
back early this morning, confirming a Kelly Delaney did
indeed live in Schenectady, New York, and worked as
an elementary-school teacher.

He wasn't sure what he'd expected the trace to re-
veal. Of course Kelly had given him her real name and
hometown. Why wouldn't she? And what other
reason could she have for searching for Mandy if it
wasn't money?

As it had the night his father went to the emergency

room, his gut told him to trust her even as his brain cautioned him to be wary. His hormones overrode both as Kelly skipped down the wide front steps of the B and B and approached the pickup.

In a V-neck tank top, blue-jean shorts that skimmed her pretty knees and sandals, she should have looked unremarkable. But a warm breeze played with her silky brown hair and the sun shone on her healthy complexion, causing her to come alive.

He was so caught up in looking at her that she yanked open the door and slung her backpack into the backseat before he could get out of the Jeep.

"Hi," she said brightly, settling into the passenger seat. "Tough morning?"

"How did you know?"

"You don't strike me as somebody who's usually late, not that I'm complaining. I know how kids can slow you down."

"You have kids?" The possibility that she was married hadn't occurred to him before now.

"Oh, yeah," she said. "Twenty-two of them."

"What?" he sputtered.

"I'm a teacher," she said with a laugh, confirming what he already knew. "I think of all my students as my kids."

Chase waited for a break in traffic that had grown heavier thanks to the Fourth of July holiday and pulled into the street, suddenly awash in curiosity about her. "It sounds like you enjoy teaching."

"I love it." She pronounced each of the three words distinctly, lending them more weight. "I love kids, period. Their innocence. Their joy. Their eagerness to learn. I feel energized when I'm around them, I guess because I'm seeing the world through their eyes."

"I feel that way around Toby." He was constantly amazed at how quickly the child had taken up space in his heart. "Don't get me wrong, I love going to work—especially because I'm not a salesman anymore—but sometimes I'd rather stay home and play with him."

"Perfectly understandable," she said. "But what did you mean about being a salesman?"

"I wasn't sure what I wanted to do with my life, so I majored in business in college," he said. "My first job was selling office equipment."

"How did you become a forest ranger?"

"I did a cold call one day at the Pennsylvania Game Commission office. A notice was posted on the bulletin board about a need for wildlife conservation officers so I decided to apply. The rest is history."

The hour's drive to Allentown passed swiftly, with his vague suspicions about Kelly slowly fading as the conversation flowed. He talked about the challenges of maintaining a home office and patrolling an area of three-hundred-and-fifty square miles, and she entertained him with stories about her students.

"One little boy was the ring bearer at his uncle's wedding," she said. "He brought a plastic ring to school and asked one of the girls to marry him. When she said no, he started to sob. After I dried his tears, he asked if I would marry him."

"What did you say?"

"That if I was still single, we could talk about it again when he had grown up."

"I think I'm jealous." Chase meant the comment to be tongue in cheek. He slanted her a look. Their eyes met and held, and something infinitesimal changed between them. He realized he'd just admitted he was attracted to her. Unless he was mistaken, she felt the same.

She broke their charged gaze and launched into another story, as if nothing had happened. He vowed to see that it didn't. He definitely was not in the market to get involved with anyone so soon after Mandy.

A collection of tents appeared before long, signaling that they'd arrived at the craft show.

They found a parking spot in a grassy field, then walked through the makeshift lot to the area where the craftsmen had set up, with Chase being careful not to get too close to her. The temperature was still moderate, but the air was humid.

A lady selling handcrafted soap that looked and smelled like chocolate told them the jewelry makers were set up at the far end of the fair. She described Helene Heffinger as a small bleached blonde with a big attitude.

En route they passed a cornucopia of crafts for sale, from custom-designed tote bags to whimsical pincushions to hand-stitched doll clothing. If somebody could dream it up, a crafter was hawking it.

Now that Chase was attuned to Kelly, he noticed little things about her. The delicacy of her profile. The way her hair rustled in the warm breeze. The eagerness in her step as they approached the jewelry section.

The only bleached blonde wore a bright red top, a flowing white skirt and red high-top tennis shoes. She perched on a tall stool above backdrops of black velvet displaying her creations. Deep lines bracketed her eyes and mouth, labeling her a smoker.

Kelly made a beeline for her and reached her first, pulling the photo they'd brought along of Mandy from her purse. She sounded almost breathless when she asked, "Are you Helene Heffinger?"

The woman peered at her above small wire-rimmed glasses as though deciding whether Kelly was worthy of an answer. Definitely not a born saleswoman, Chase thought. "Yeah," the woman intoned.

Kelly hurriedly introduced herself and Chase, then held out the photo. "We're looking for a woman who might be one of your customers."

"What did she do?" Heffinger demanded.

"Do?" Kelly seemed taken aback by the confrontational question. "She didn't *do* anything."

"Is she a missing person then?"

"Well, no." Kelly said.

"Then she must owe you money," Heffinger said. "Why else would you be looking for her?"

"It has nothing to do with money," Kelly interjected, the lie pouring off her like water over a fall. She gazed directly at the jewelry-maker, her eyes clear, her voice earnest. If Chase had been on the receiving end of that denial, he would have believed her. "I'm not the one who needs to find her. Chase is. I'm helping him."

Heffinger's gaze shifted to Chase, who was prompted into replying, "She's an ex-girlfriend."

"She left her baby with him," Kelly added while Chase was deciding how much detail tell Heffinger. "His name is Toby, and he's only a year old."

Chase might not have shared his story so baldly, but had to admit the strategy paid off. Heffinger definitely seemed interested. "So you think something might have happened to her?"

"Yes! We're worried about her," Kelly said, another lie spilling easily from her lips. "We just want to make sure she's all right."

"Why come to me?" Heffinger asked.

"We thought you might keep a mailing list of your customers. We're not sure where she lived before she moved in with Chase. If we had an address, we could check with neighbors to see if she reached out to them."

Heffinger extended a hand, wordlessly asking for a second look at the sketch. "What's her name?"

"Mandy Smith," Kelly answered. "But she might be going by Amanda. She might even be using a different last name."

Chase remained silent, watching Kelly in action, his doubts about her resurrecting. She was now telling the truth, but seemed no less sincere than she had when she lied.

"Why do you think she's one of my customers?" Heffinger asked.

Kelly produced the necklace. "This was hers."

Heffinger fingered the jewelry, turning the necklace over and scowling at the broken clasp before handing it back. "I guarantee my work. She should have brought it back for a refund."

"Then you do remember her?" Kelly asked, audible hope in her voice.

"A woman didn't buy this from me. A man did. I remember because he gave me a drawing of a necklace and talked me into making something that looked like it."

Chase figured he'd kept silent long enough. "How long ago was this?"

"At least a year and a half," Heffinger said. "Maybe more."

"Do you remember his name?"

"What do I look like? An elephant?" She huffed. "Like I said, lots of people buy jewelry from me."

"Do you keep copies of your receipts?"

"'Course I do." Heffinger sounded affronted. "But I only take cash."

"So there's no way to know who bought this necklace from you," Chase finished.

"Not unless I wrote down his name and phone number on the receipt so I could call and tell him when the necklace was finished."

That sounded like a distinct possibility to Chase. He dug in the pocket of his khaki shorts and pulled out a business card. "Here's my cell number and e-mail address. If you come across that phone number, would you contact us?"

"I can't promise nothing," she said, but took the card. "It'd take a while to go through my records."

"One more thing," Chase said, continuing before Heffinger could get even testier. "Could you help me pick out a piece of jewelry for my babysitter?"

Heffinger suggested a bracelet of colored stones that cost well more than Chase wanted to spend, but to increase the chances that she'd contact them he took her recommendation.

"It'd mean a lot if you checked your records, Ms. Heffinger," Kelly said after Chase paid for the bracelet. "If we can find that man, maybe we can find Mandy. Like I said, we just want to make sure she's okay."

Kelly sounded earnest, the way she had when she told her original story about wanting to return the broken necklace and then again when relating how Mandy had stolen her ATM card.

Since she'd easily twisted the truth to bend Helene Heffinger to her will, the question remained whether Chase could believe anything she said.

CHAPTER SEVEN

KELLY TRIED NOT TO GET discouraged as she and Chase walked away from Helene Heffinger. The jeweler had said she'd check her records, not that she wouldn't help. But the reality was that, even if Heffinger had information about the man who'd bought the necklace on file, it might not help them find Mandy.

In retrospect, Kelly acknowledged that the lead had been a long shot. She'd been emotionally and physically spent after talking to the bartender at the Blue Haven and had let herself hope that Heffinger would recognize Mandy and provide her new address. A pipe dream.

She wished now that she'd spent the latter part of yesterday searching for fresh clues instead of succumbing to exhaustion. So far she was getting nowhere while her preliminary hearing got closer with each passing day.

"You're a very good liar," Chase said.

Her step faltered, her defenses going up like a brick wall. She'd felt so comfortable with Chase during the drive to the craft fair that she'd let herself forget he was in law enforcement.

She'd let herself become attracted to him.

Who was she trying to fool? One of the reasons she'd

asked him to team up with her had been that she was already attracted to him. Far too much.

"I only said what I did to get Ms. Heffinger to help us," she explained. "She wouldn't have helped if I told her Mandy owed me money."

He stuck his hands in the pockets of his shorts, not looking at her as they weaved through the burgeoning crowd. Most of the women they passed, and quite a few of the men, gave him second looks. She thought it was mostly because they could tell from his carriage he was a man of substance.

Fear that he'd discover her true motives wasn't paramount in her mind, she realized. She was afraid of him thinking poorly of her. It was a hell of a thing, but there it was.

"It made more sense to tell her why *you* were looking for Mandy," Kelly continued. "Your story's more sympathetic."

He said nothing. The easy camaraderie of the morning had vanished as completely as the smoke from a barbecue grill.

A half dozen food vendors had set up around a flat, grassy area populated with portable tables and chairs. "I need to get to work as soon as we get back so how about an early lunch?" Chase said as they approached the area. "I'll buy."

"That's not necessary," Kelly said.

"I thought you were short on cash." The inflection in his voice hinted he no longer believed that was the case, doubt she'd brought on herself. He was both right and wrong. Mandy hadn't been the one to clean her out her savings account, but the money Kelly had withdrawn was disappearing fast.

"I am a little short," she said.

"Then I'll treat."

After they ordered, she followed him to a table where he set down their tray of food. The silence between them was so pronounced, the popping of their soda tops sounded like gunfire. He bit into his cheeseburger, but she ignored her chicken sandwich, still chewing on her lie.

The lie that had slipped from her as easily as air from her lungs. The lie that met with his disapproval. But couldn't he see that all lies weren't the same, that there were times when lying was necessary? At one period in her life, she'd viewed them as survival tools.

"Lying isn't always wrong, you know," she said.

He set down his burger on his paper plate and looked her full in the face for the first time since they'd left Helene Heffinger. "How so?"

She fidgeted, picked up her soda can, put it down without taking a drink. How could she make him understand? "What would you say if a woman asked if her jeans made her look fat?"

He folded his hands over his chest, the line of his mouth as uncompromising as his posture. "If she's asking, she already knows they make her look fat."

She sighed. "Then what about a lie to protect the innocent?"

He gave a quick shake of his head. "I'm not following."

Like him, she didn't touch her food. She was too busy concentrating on a way to sway Chase from his rigid view of the world. She slowly came up with a scenario to illustrate her point. "What if your dad was arrested for murder?"

"Never happen," he said quickly. "My dad's not capable of hurting anyone."

"You're sure of that?"

His eyes narrowed. "Positive."

"Then what if it was a case of mistaken identity? Your dad tells the cops he's innocent, but they insist they have the right guy." She kept on, even though the situation was uncomfortably close to her personal catastrophe, hoping to get Chase to see things in a different light. "If you say your dad was with you at the time of the murder, he goes free and nobody knows you lied."

"I'd know."

She felt her jaw drop. "You'd let your dad go to prison?"

"I'd tell the truth and then try like hell to dig up proof that he was innocent."

Chase had far too much faith in the truth. The facts hadn't kept Kelly out of jail. "In my world, everything isn't so clear cut. Sometimes lying is a necessary evil."

He raised a skeptical eyebrow. "Like when you're looking for a woman who owes you money?"

No! she wanted to shout. When you're running out of leads in a desperate search to locate the only woman who can keep you out of prison.

How, she wondered, could she make him understand? She'd have to try another approach: The truth.

"I was on my sixth elementary school by the time I was twelve years old," she blurted. "I lost count of how many times I was the new kid. It wasn't easy to fit in, especially if the other kids found out I was a foster child."

She seldom revealed the way she'd grown up to anybody, even now. She hesitated, not ready to share the whole story of how her mother's arrest for murder and subsequent sentence to life without parole had landed her in the foster-care system as a frightened eight year old. But she wanted to tell him at least part of it.

"Sometimes I said my mother was a doctor and my father was a lawyer. Other times they were both architects who designed fabulous buildings. Once I said they were independently wealthy so they both just stayed home and took care of me."

He said nothing, but uncrossed his arms from his chest and leaned slightly forward, regarding her with interest rather than his previous apprehension.

"Eventually somebody always found out I was lying but by then I was already leaving, off to another foster family, another school," she said.

More and more people were stopping for lunch, filling the tables around them, their chatter growing louder and louder. Kelly barely noticed any of the commotion, so focused was she on her past.

"Did you move around from family to family your entire childhood?" he asked.

"Oh, no." She shook her head for emphasis. "I landed with Mama Rosa when I was thirteen and that's where I stayed, thank God."

"Mama Rosa?" Chase prodded.

"My foster mother. She was at least six feet tall, with deep lines on her face and this loud, gruff voice." Kelly's mind rewound to the first time she'd gazed up at the big, tough woman. "She told me right off the bat we'd be fine as long as I was straight with her. She scared me half to death, to tell you the truth."

"Did you lie to her, too?"

"At first, mostly so she wouldn't find out I didn't measure up." She'd lied about whether she'd finished her homework, the grades she'd made on her tests, if she'd done her chores. "Then one day, a couple of us were horsing around in the house. Mama Rosa had this beautiful heirloom lamp. I tripped and knocked it over. It broke into a hundred pieces."

She pressed her lips together, remembering how much her foster mother had loved the lamp and how afraid Kelly had been for her to discover who'd broken it.

"She asked who did it. I said it wasn't me. She got quiet, then this big tear dripped down her cheek. I'd never seen her cry before. I couldn't stand how much it hurt for her to lose the lamp, so I confessed." She blew out a breath. "It turned out she wasn't crying because of the broken lamp. She was crying because I'd lied to her. Again."

A man walking by their table bumped Chase's chair and apologized. He barely seemed to notice.

"What happened?" he asked.

"Nothing. She was true to her word. I'd told the truth, so I didn't get grounded." She stared down at her hands. "I never lied to her again."

She stopped short of telling him she hadn't entirely given up the behavior. Oh, she'd never cheat on her income tax or tell a lie that would hurt anybody, but she usually claimed her mother was dead. Neither was she above telling the occasional white lie. More than once, she'd claimed to have a boyfriend when someone asked her out.

"Your foster mother sounds like a remarkable woman."

"She was. After I moved in with her, she got licensed for short-term emergency care. Most of the time, there were five or six other kids living with us. It was like a revolving door."

"Where is she now?"

"She died of a brain aneurysm when I was a freshman in college." Pain lanced through her even though Mama Rosa had been dead going on six years. "One day she was fine, and the next she was gone."

He reached across the table and covered her hand with his, understanding glowing in the depths of his eyes. She realized she'd also described what happened to his mother.

"It doesn't hurt as much as it used to," she told him. "She'd want me to be happy she lived instead of sad that she's no longer here. She taught me so much I feel a part of her lives on in me."

"She taught you it's wrong to lie," he stated.

"Yeah. She wouldn't have approved of what I told Helene Heffinger today." She voiced her conclusion aloud. "Which means you were right. I shouldn't have lied to her."

"We all do things we shouldn't," he said. "But not everybody admits it when they make a mistake."

Chase would own up to his miscues. He was a stand-up guy, a do-the-right-thing kind of guy. He wasn't the sort of guy who deserved to be lied to.

The cell phone clipped to Chase's belt rang, interrupting them. She listened to his end of the conversation, figuring there was some problem with Teresa.

"Just do what you need to do and don't worry about it," he said in a calm, sure voice. "I'll manage."

Chase finished the call, then swore under his breath.

"Is everything okay?" she asked.

"Not really. Teresa's daughter called from the emergency room in Philly. Her three year old fell and hit her head. Her husband's out of town so she left the two year old with a neighbor. She asked if Teresa could come right away."

"What about Toby?"

"That's why Teresa called. Her neighbor will watch him until we get back to town, but then I need to find a babysitter for the rest of the day."

"I'll do it," Kelly offered instantly.

"Are you sure?" he said. "It's going to be crazy tonight because of the holiday. I'll probably help the police patrol for DUIs after the sun goes down so it could be a late night."

"Then I'll stay the night at your place," she said. "You'd be doing me a favor, too. The B and B is booked for the weekend so it would save me finding another hotel."

"I wasn't sure you were staying in town."

She couldn't go back to Wenona. Not yet. Not when she wasn't much closer to locating Mandy than she had been when she left. "For the time being."

"How much did Mandy steal from you anyway?" he asked, his expression curious.

My good name and possibly my freedom, Kelly thought.

"A good deal," she said, skirting an untruth. "Let me do this, Chase. I'd like to help you."

"Okay," he said. "Thanks. This is perfect. You can sleep in Mandy's room."

"Mandy's room?" Kelly parroted, tact forgotten.

"That's right," he said. "She had her own room."

Kelly longed to know why they hadn't shared a room, but it wasn't any of her business. She should be thanking him instead of questioning him, especially because she might find a clue as to where Mandy had gone in the house. "That'd be great."

"Then it's settled." He smiled at her, obviously not having taken offense at her question. Her stomach lurched.

She'd told him the story about growing up in foster care to explain why she sometimes felt it necessary to lie, but then they'd gotten on the tangent of Mama Rosa. It seemed she'd inadvertently convinced him she was inherently trustworthy.

She meant to try her best to be truthful from here on out, but she couldn't take back the lies she'd already told. Not until they found Mandy.

She felt a stab in the region of her heart, but it was neither a heart attack or heartburn. It was despair.

Because, considering the sort of man he was, by then he'd probably never forgive her.

WHAT A DIFFERENCE THIRTY-SIX hours made, Chase thought as he quietly made his way through the downstairs of the dark house Friday night.

When he'd returned from the hospital in the wee hours of Thursday morning, he'd been anxious about his decision to leave Toby with a woman he'd just met. Earlier today, after Kelly had flip-flopped her story about why she was searching for Mandy and then lied to Helene Heffinger, he'd questioned Kelly's credibility.

But tonight, even though there was still much he didn't know about Kelly, he experienced no such qualms.

It could be because of the love and respect in her voice when she'd shared the tale about her principled foster mother. Or because of how great she was with Toby.

He wasn't exactly sure why, but the wall of suspicion he'd been erecting had come crumbling down.

It had been silly but tonight, as he'd patrolled the waters and then the highways, he'd thought about going home.

To Kelly.

"Fool," he called himself.

She was passing through Indigo Springs and would soon be gone. Even if they had the sort of relationship where she'd be eagerly waiting for him to come home, it was just after midnight. She wouldn't be waiting now.

He flipped on the light switch, blinked, then blinked again. There at the kitchen table, her hands wrapped around a glass of milk, was Kelly.

"Hey," he said. "I didn't see you there."

She grimaced. "You weren't supposed to. That's why I didn't turn on the light."

He advanced a step. She was dressed for bed in an oversized T-shirt that he found oddly provocative, and her hair was charmingly disheveled. "Why exactly are you sitting in the dark?"

She sighed, then held up...an Oreo?

"I raided your cabinet. When I can't sleep, milk and cookies are the only thing that work for me."

He grinned. "That's your deep, dark secret?"

"Don't laugh. It's a bad habit. Everybody knows whatever you eat before bed goes straight to your hips."

He imagined her hips swaying gently as she walked. "Then keep eating those Oreos because your hips are perfect."

Her eyes met his and she blushed before looking away quickly. He couldn't remember the last time a woman had gotten flustered when he'd delivered a compliment and found it oddly sweet. It caused her to seem younger than her years and lent her an innocence that made his previous suspicions seem crazy.

He wondered how she'd react if he remarked on how much he liked her T-shirt but decided instead to try to put her at ease. "You might try warming up the milk and adding honey next time. It tastes awful, but it helps with insomnia."

She exhaled, her body visibly relaxing. She probably didn't know that the material of the T-shirt clung to her, outlining breasts that were high, firm and just the right size.

"I thought people with babies were so exhausted they fell asleep as soon as their heads hit the pillow," she said.

"I'm lucky. Toby usually sleeps through the night so I'm as prone to insomnia as the next guy." He took the chair next to her and stole her last Oreo. "Why can't you sleep? It wasn't Toby, was it?"

"Oh, no. He was an angel. He went to sleep hours ago." She held up the receiving end of Toby's baby monitor. He could hear Toby's deep, even breaths. "Since then, he's been sleeping like, well, a baby."

She laughed, the sound low and pleasant, then asked, "Did you hear from Teresa?"

"Yeah. Her granddaughter's fine. She didn't even have a concussion."

"That's good. How about you? How are you doing? Was it a tough night?"

"Tough enough," he said. "People use the holidays as an excuse to drink too much. I hauled a couple of boaters into jail this afternoon, then had another DUI arrest tonight."

"I'm glad you got 'em," she said.

"Now are you gonna tell me why you can't sleep?" He popped the entire Oreo into his mouth. She was right—the cookies weren't nearly as good without milk. She pushed her glass toward him, wordlessly offering exactly what he wanted.

"Thanks." He guzzled some milk, finding as he swallowed that he didn't need words to know what was on her mind, either. "It's because of Mandy, isn't it?"

"It's hard not to think about her when I'm sleeping in her room. That reminds me. I found this wadded up between the nightstand and the bed." She unfolded a small T-shirt and held it up. It was pink with the image of a turtle standing on its hind legs, its front legs outstretched, its mouth open in glee. "Was it Mandy's?"

"I don't recognize it, but probably," he said. "Why?"

"I guess I figured it might be a clue, but I'm grasping at straws." She fingered the neck of the T-shirt. "It doesn't even have a tag."

She looked down at the table, then up at him, her eyes troubled. "Would you mind if I asked you a question?"

"Depends on the question," he said, although at the moment he'd probably tell her anything.

"Did you know what kind of person she was?"

"You mean, did I know she was capable of stealing?" He thought of Mandy assuring him she was on the Pill, telling him she was pregnant with his baby, insisting she'd had a miscarriage. "I think Mandy is capable of a great many things."

"Then why were you with her?"

There were two lights in the kitchen, but he'd only turned on the one beside the stove. Kelly was mostly in shadows, the fact that he couldn't see her face clearly making it easier to answer. "Because she told me she was pregnant."

She shook her head. "No. I meant before that. Why were you two together at all?"

"It was only for one night."

"Oh," she said, as though she understood.

He frowned. By telling her the truth, he'd misled her. "I'm not in the habit of having one-night stands. I like to get to know a woman before I jump into bed with her."

"Then why…" Her voice trailed off. "Never mind, it's none of my business."

She was right. The reason he'd slept with Mandy mere hours after meeting her was intensely personal, something he never intended to share with another person, but he could tell her at least part of it.

"She was fun and funny and being with her took my mind off my problems." He kneaded his forehead. "Hell, that sounded like an excuse. I didn't mean it to be."

"So when she got pregnant, you decided to marry her?"

"Who told you that?" he asked, although he could guess the answer.

"Your father."

He was glad he hadn't told his father about Mandy faking the miscarriage. "Like I've said before, my father talks too much. But, yeah, I would have married her. Bizarre when you realize how little I know about her."

"Is that why you haven't been able to find her?"

"That's right. I mean, I'm in law enforcement. You'd think I could track down the woman I used to live with, but she didn't leave a trail I can find."

"Your father said she wasn't a good mother."

"What else did he say?"

"That she didn't try to make friends and that she wasn't your type." She wrinkled her nose. "At least I think he said she wasn't your type, but that could be my conclusion."

"Oh, yeah?" He raised his eyebrows. "Suppose you tell me what my type is."

"Let me think about that." A corner of her mouth quirked. It was a very pretty mouth, the lower lip slightly more lush than the upper one. "Well, she'd obviously have to love children because of Toby."

"Obviously," he agreed.

"She'd have to share your values. Truth. Justice. The American way." She was teasing him, her eyes sparkling. "I see you with a nester. You'd never be happy with a flighty party girl."

"Right again. Anything else?"

"It wouldn't hurt if she thought your dad was funny."

They smiled at each other, the darkened house and

the late hour causing the shared joke to seem intimate, but her assessment wasn't far off the mark. Chase wasn't in the market for a relationship after the mess he'd gotten into with Mandy, but if he were it would be easier if the woman got along with his father. And shared his values. And loved children.

And turned him on even when she wasn't trying, just by sitting in the dark, wearing a T-shirt, with a plate of Oreos and a glass of milk.

"You know who you just described, don't you?" he asked in a low voice.

She shook her head.

"You."

"I didn't," she denied.

She polished off the rest of her milk and stood. The T-shirt fell to the middle of her thighs, leaving her legs bare. He could see the silhouette of her figure through the thin material. His mouth went dry.

Her brow knitted and he imagined she was replaying what she'd said. "Okay, maybe I did describe myself. Then I must've been wrong about your type."

"I wouldn't say that." He stood up, too. He'd taken off his shoes when he came in the house, but he still topped her by five or six inches. Taking her empty glass, he set it on the counter, his eyes never leaving her lovely face. "I think you got my type exactly right."

Her throat constricted as she swallowed. She was nervous, he realized. Like her blush, her slightly uneven breathing made her more attractive. He should be exhausted considering the hour but his senses came screamingly alive.

Her eyes were huge in her pale face. Slowly he pushed the fingers of his right hand through her hair, cradling the back of her scalp. "I like your hair."

"Thank you," she said formally.

He grinned, charmed by her response.

With the index finger of his left hand, he traced the slope of her nose, pausing halfway down. "I like this little bump."

She didn't move. She didn't even blink.

He lowered his finger, exploring the indentation between the bottom of her nose and her mouth. "And this little crevice."

"It's called a philtrum," she said, her voice breathless. "I only know that because someone mentioned it once on a television show."

"Okay, then I like your philtrum," he said, testing the word. His fingers moved lower, to trace the outline of her lips. "But I love your mouth."

His lips replaced his fingers, molding themselves to the sweet curve of her lips. She accepted the kiss, standing on tiptoe, anchoring her hands on his shoulders. Sensation swamped him, his body going instantly hard despite the kiss being almost chaste. Although their mouths were locked, inches separated their bodies.

She was the one to deepen the kiss, flicking her tongue lightly over the tip of his. He groaned, taking control of the kiss, switching from chaste to hot in an instant. She kept pace, twining her arms around his neck, plastering herself against his body so she couldn't miss his arousal.

Their mouths mated, the way he wanted to join with her. And why not? They were two consenting adults with the house to themselves. His initial reaction after Mandy had played him for a fool was to vow not to let any other woman take advantage of him, but it wasn't in his nature to blame one woman's actions on another. Kelly wasn't Mandy.

Kelly made him feel things no other woman had.

Wonderful things.

The tinny sound of a baby crying intruded on his consciousness. The baby monitor. Toby. With great difficulty he called upon his willpower and pulled back. Kelly gazed at him, her lips parted, her face flushed, her eyes slightly glazed. He'd never seen her look more desirable.

"What's wrong?" she rasped.

The sobs emanating from the baby monitor answered for him.

He leaned his forehead against hers, trying to summon the strength to leave her. "I have to get him."

"I know you do." Her lips curved in a shaky smile. "Then you should get some sleep. Don't you have work tomorrow morning?"

"I do have work," he said, "but I don't need sleep."

She laughed softly.

"Go comfort Toby, then get some rest." Her breath was warm and sweet against his lips. "It's tough to let you go, but it's just as well. I was forgetting that I like to get to know a man before I jump into bed with him."

He'd said something similar to her just moments ago. The philosophy usually made perfect sense, but not in this case. The hell of it was that he was absolutely certain Kelly felt the same.

Toby's cries grew more insistent, rendering the point

moot. They wouldn't be resuming their lovemaking tonight. Disappointment crashed through him with the force of an avalanche.

"Go to Toby," she urged. "I understand."

She wouldn't be his type if she didn't, which made climbing the stairs away from her all that much harder.

CHAPTER EIGHT

"ONE. TWO. THREE. THROW!"

"Catch those suckers!"

"Don't let them splat!"

Squeals of delight and bursts of laughter pierced the late-afternoon air. The sounds emanated from the downtown park where two lines of children faced each other on a grassy field at a distance of about six feet.

Kelly had to give credit to Chase and the other man shouting encouragement. They really knew how to get the kids excited about an egg toss.

"Get ready for the next toss!" Chase's partner yelled.

"Remember to cradle those puppies." Chase demonstrated the fine points of how to catch an egg by cupping his hands with his palms facing skyward. "Soft hands are the key."

Kelly smiled to herself. If Chase were competing, she'd put her money on him. Even though he had the slightly calloused hands of an outdoorsman, she knew from firsthand experience that they could be very soft.

"Ready! Set! Go!" the other man yelled loudly.

Eggs flew all over the field, some finding their marks, others hitting the ground and smashing, still others breaking apart in the hands of the young participants.

The competition was part of the Indigo Springs Fourth of July festival, which had begun early that morning with a 5K race, continued at noon with a reading of the Declaration of Independence, then really got rolling in the late afternoon with a parade down Main Street.

Charlie had returned from his fishing trip just before noon, expressing little surprise to find Kelly at the house babysitting Toby.

He'd taken it for granted that Kelly would accompany him and Toby to the festival. So after the baby's nap, they'd packed Toby and his assorted paraphernalia in the car, arriving just in time to watch the marching bands, floats, motorcycle cops and dancing teams commemorate the Fourth.

The children's games portion of the festival was currently underway, with dinner and live music to follow. The entire event would be capped off with a fireworks show that event organizers promised would be spectacular.

"Chins up!" Chase told the disappointed duos who'd allowed their eggs to break. "You can't let a little egg get you down!"

Even some of the disqualified children laughed at his comment. It was easy for Kelly to see why the festival organizers had deputized Chase and his friend to run the children's games.

She leaned closer to Charlie on the bench they'd been lucky enough to find vacant. Not only was it in the shade, but the spot had a clear view of the field. Toby sat on Charlie's lap,

"Who's the guy with Chase?" She indicated Chase's tall, darkly handsome companion. With his very short hair and athletic build, he looked almost as good as Chase. But not quite.

"That's Michael Donahue," Charlie answered. "He's in the construction business with the Pollocks. I think you might have met his fiancée, Sara. She's a lawyer. Office on Main Street."

"Oh, yeah." Kelly took a quick look around, feeling herself relax when she didn't spot Sara. In other circumstances she would have tried to befriend the lawyer, but Sara had been openly suspicious when Kelly had questioned her about Mandy.

"Michael's great-aunt is on the festival committee," Charlie continued. "When nobody stepped up to run the children's games, she volunteered Michael. Poor Mike was so nervous about doing it himself that he bribed Chase to help him."

"Bribed? How?"

Charlie chuckled. "He offered Chase a hundred bucks to be his wingman."

"And Chase took his money?"

"Of course not. But Chase did get Michael to promise to pour us a new driveway."

"For free?"

"Chase let Michael think so, but you know my boy. He'd never take advantage of a friend like that."

Kelly did indeed have a hard time picturing Chase manipulating the situation to serve his driveway needs, but something about the story didn't compute. "Why would Chase need to be bribed? He looks like he's having the time of his life."

"That's the really funny thing," Charlie said. "Sara had already lined up Chase to help before Michael approached him, only Michael didn't know it."

Toby reached out and batted Kelly in the nose, smiling as though he was playing the carnival game Whack a Mole and her nose was the mole.

"No, no, sweetheart. We don't play patty-cake with noses." Kelly rubbed her smarting nose. With hand-eye coordination like that, she thought, Toby might be a ringer at future egg tosses.

The participants in the event had been dropping like the eggs they were tossing as Kelly and Charlie talked. Only two very eager teams remained.

"Didn't that blond kid win the sack race?" Kelly indicated a lithe, handsome boy who had a knack for catching an egg.

"Yep. That's Timmy Waverly. Eleven years old and already one of the best athletes in town." Charlie inclined his head toward a cluster of parents in the distance. "See the blond guy with the chiseled features. He was a pole vaulter at Penn State. He's Timmy's dad."

Timmy's dad was also the man who'd waylaid Kelly when she'd gone to get some freshly squeezed lemonade during the Frisbee throw. He'd introduced himself as Jim Waverly, then barely took a breath before asking if she'd like to meet him for a drink sometime, the fastest come-on Kelly had ever experienced. She'd politely declined.

The two remaining pairs vying for the egg-toss championship title took another giant step backward. The four children practically vibrated with excitement in anticipation of the command to let the eggs fly.

Charlie paid little attention to the drama on the field, as he had all day. His eyes roamed the crowd, even though the cast of characters hadn't changed much since the children's games began. A throng of young mothers were standing together, some of them openly staring at Kelly and Charlie.

"Are you looking for somebody?" Kelly asked.

"No!" Charlie said quickly.

"Really?"

"Okay, you got me." He sounded sheepish. "But it's no big mystery. Teresa said she'd be here and I don't see her. She's a family friend."

Amid more squeals, the two pairs vying for the win successfully completed their tosses and catches. The smallest girl, who wore pigtails and couldn't have weighed more than sixty pounds, did a celebratory jumping jack.

"If you're talking about Teresa Jessup, she's probably still in Philadelphia with her daughter and grandchildren," Kelly said.

"Teresa's in Philadelphia?" Charlie sat up straighter. This time Toby tried to bop his nose, but Charlie dodged and the baby missed. Charlie didn't even bother to reprimand him. "When did she go to Philadelphia?"

"Yesterday. Her granddaughter fell and hit her head and went to the emergency room. At first they thought it might be a concussion but she's fine."

"Is Teresa still there?"

"As far as I know," Kelly peered at him, wondering whether Teresa was more than a casual family friend.

"Don't let that little bugger drop!" Chase yelled, switching Kelly's attention back to the egg toss.

"Get it in the hands!" shouted Michael Donahue.

Both children on the receiving ends of the high-arcing throws from their teammates followed the directions to the letter, catching the eggs cleanly. The pigtailed girl beamed but Timmy Waverly grimaced. He opened his hands. Egg yolk dripped onto the grass.

Letting out a high-pitched shriek of triumph, the girl held her unbroken egg in the air.

Chase whooped. Michael raised both his arms and the little girl and her equally young partner jumped up and down as if their legs were pogo sticks.

"Great job, everybody!" Chase yelled, awarding the participants with a round of applause. "Now on to the pie-eating contest!"

While Michael herded the children to the outdoor pavilion where the next event was being held, Chase jogged to the shady spot where Kelly sat with Charlie and Toby. He had on the same bright orange T-shirt as the other festival volunteers, but the color didn't fare so badly when worn over a very nicely put together chest.

Because Chase had already left for work by the time Kelly woke that morning, this was the first time she'd been within six feet of him since last night's kiss.

She'd half convinced herself she'd imagined the excitement that tingled through her whenever he was near, but the thrill was still there.

"I'm coming for you, Toby!" he cried before plucking the giggling boy from Charlie's lap and giving him a smacking kiss on the cheek.

Kelly thought Toby was a very lucky baby.

"You and your friend run a mean competition," Kelly said. "Those kids are having a great time."

Chase smiled at Kelly over the baby's head. His brown eyes were warm, the smile intimate even though they weren't alone.

"The kids aren't the only ones having fun," he said, "but I'm a little worried about the pie-eating. Seems Michael promised a couple of the kids we'd take them on."

Charlie chuckled. "That should be entertaining. Aren't the pie shells filled with whipped cream?"

"Yes. And you can't use your hands." Chase rolled his eyes and handed Toby back to his father.

"Mr. Chase! Mr. Chase!" The two girls who'd won the egg toss ran up to them and flanked Chase, each taking one of his hands and tugging. The pigtailed girl was more persistent. "Come on. We're going to be late."

Chase winked at Kelly before he let the two girls drag him off, calling over his shoulder, "Gotta go and make a fool of myself."

"This I have to see," Kelly remarked to Charlie. "Are you coming?"

He hesitated. "I think I'll just sit here in the shade a while longer with Toby."

"I can take him off your hands if you need a break," Kelly offered.

"You better not."

She picked up on a strange vibe in his voice. "Why not?"

"Louise Wiesneski," he said. "She's the librarian who asked Chase a bunch of questions about Mandy the other day. She's over by that tall pine tree. She's been staring at us."

Kelly turned her head in the direction he'd indicated, but couldn't pick out which woman was Louise Wiesneski. "A lot of people seem to be staring at us."

"They're wondering who you are and where Mandy is," Charlie said in a soft voice. "For Chase's sake, don't give them anything to gossip about. In fact, it might be best if you let them think you and Mandy are related. You sure look enough alike."

Kelly chewed on her bottom lip, mulling over his suggestion. "Chase won't like it if I lie to his friends."

"He'll like it even less if people start speculating that Mandy abandoned her baby. Then he'll get it into his fool head that he has to go to DPW."

"I thought he was going to do that anyway."

"Not if I can talk him out of it," Charlie said. "We don't know if DPW would let us keep Toby so why ask for trouble? We'll find Mandy eventually. If it takes a couple of months, it takes a couple of months."

Kelly nodded her agreement because Charlie's argument made sense. It seemed highly likely that Mandy wasn't coming back for Toby, but nobody could be sure of that. If Chase could manage to stay away from DPW, he had the luxury of time to find Mandy.

Kelly didn't.

She told Charlie and Toby she'd catch up with them later, then headed for the pavilion. While she walked, she chastised herself for forgetting, even for a second, why she was in Indigo Springs.

She should be spending every waking moment searching for clues instead of letting herself be lulled into the false notion that she could fit into Chase's life.

Since yesterday, when she'd searched the bedroom where Mandy had once slept and found nothing except that useless T-shirt, she hadn't done a thing to find the other woman.

That needed to change. Immediately.

One of the young mothers who'd been openly staring at Kelly was walking toward the pavilion ahead of her. Kelly considered picking up her pace so she could find out whether the woman had known Mandy, then remembered Charlie's warning.

The woman could be Louise Wiesneski, the librarian. How could Kelly question her when her inquiries might bring Chase trouble?

Just as Kelly made the decision to hang back, the woman turned and spotted her. She slowed, waiting for Kelly to catch up. Tall and reed-thin, she had frizzy blond hair she wore in a ponytail.

"Hi. I'm Edie Clark," she said, and Kelly relaxed. Edie resumed walking when Kelly fell in step beside her. "You're new in town, aren't you?"

Something about the quasi-casual way in which she framed the question warned Kelly that Edie could be as nosy as Louise Wiesneski. She decided not to provide the woman with her last name. "I'm Kelly, and I'm just visiting."

"I knew I hadn't seen you around before when I noticed you over there with Charlie Bradford and the little boy. Is he your nephew?"

Edie evidently hadn't heard about Kelly showing the sketch of Mandy around town. Just as obviously, she was fishing for information that she'd probably turn around and share with her friends. Kelly needed to tread carefully, exactly as Charlie had advised.

Kelly smiled pleasantly. "Why do you ask?"

"Why?" Edie seemed surprised by the question. "Because you look just like Mandy except for the hair color. Some of us have been wondering if you're sisters."

It was unlucky for Kelly that Mandy hadn't kept the dyed red shade. If the kidnapper had been a redhead, the eyewitness would have been far less likely to misidentify Kelly.

"We get that a lot." Kelly left her connection to Mandy purposely vague, but Edie nodded as though she'd gotten confirmation of her assumption.

"Thank goodness the two of you are related." Edie abruptly stopped walking. Kelly did, too. "Now I can admit I was taken aback when I thought maybe you and Chase... Well, never mind that now. Not that I don't believe what's good for the goose is good for the gander."

"Excuse me," Kelly said, "but I don't know what you're talking about."

Edie glanced left then right before lowering her voice to a stage whisper. "I really shouldn't tell you."

In other circumstances, Kelly wouldn't ask. Edie was

clearly a terrible gossip, the kind of woman Kelly tried to avoid. But if Edie was privy to information about Mandy, Kelly needed to know what it was.

"Since Mandy would probably confide in you herself, I guess it won't hurt." Edie looked around again, found nobody within hearing range, then continued in the hushed tones that were as loud as most speaking voices. "Mandy was seeing somebody."

Kelly hadn't expected that. "Somebody here in town?"

"Oh, yes. And him being married yet." Edie pursed her lips and shook her head, as though she was the one who'd been wronged.

"Who is he?"

Edie acted as though she was debating whether to share her information, then made a face and sucked in her breath. "Jim Waverly."

Kelly instantly recognized the name of the father of the young athlete who'd been a finalist in the egg toss. But Waverly had made it a point to tell her he wasn't married when he'd hit on her. "I thought he was divorced."

Edie's eyes widened and her mouth dropped open. "You know who he is then?"

Kelly thought it best not to provide Edie's curiosity with any more fuel so she simply nodded.

"I guess it's hard not to notice a good-looking guy like Jim," Edie said, then continued when Kelly said nothing. "He's divorced now, but the divorce only became final last week. Besides, even if he wasn't in a relationship at the time of the affair, Mandy was."

Mandy hadn't been in a good relationship, but Kelly knew better than to share that tidbit with Edie. She wished she'd known about the alleged affair between Mandy and Jim Waverly before the festival. That would have been reason enough to accept Waverly's offer of a drink.

"Mom!" A freckled girl of about seven years old who'd competed in the egg toss rushed over to them, her eyes bright. "Hurry! The pie-eating contest is gonna start!"

"Excuse me," Edie said to Kelly, laughing as the excitable little girl led her by the hand over to the pavilion.

Kelly followed at a slower pace, her own eagerness to watch the contest dimmed. Her encounter with Edie had reinforced the fact that Kelly was merely pretending to be part of the Indigo Springs community.

She was no longer the woman who'd tagged along to the festival because a single, wonderful kiss had caused her to want to experience what it felt like to be part of Chase's world.

She was a woman on a mission.

And that mission was to corner Jim Waverly and find out if he knew where Mandy was.

CHASE USUALLY ENJOYED the music at the Fourth of July festival.

The high-school band, the color-guard ensemble, the local rock group with dreams of hitting it big. They *all* sounded infinitely better when listened to outdoors in the company of friends, especially when the weather cooperated.

Tonight, with the temperature hovering around seventy degrees and with four of his friends and Toby spread out beside him on a giant blanket, Chase could have been tone-deaf.

"Who is Kelly talking to?" Sara Brenneman craned her neck to get a better view through the sea of people in the downtown park. On the amphitheater stage, the musicians scheduled to perform next set up for their show. Restless children chased one another around an adjacent field.

Toby was more tired than restless. Chase had put the baby in his combination carrier-car seat when his eyes reached half-mast. They were well below that now, the whites barely visible.

In addition to Toby and Sara, Chase's group included Michael Donahue and Johnny and Penelope Pollock. Johnny's arm was slung around his bride of a little more than a month.

"That's Timmy Waverly's dad." Chase didn't need to turn around to provide the answer to the question of who was monopolizing Kelly. Neither did he particularly want to talk about the man. "First in the sack race, but runner-up in the egg toss and three-legged race. The kid's a natural."

"Only in the solo events," Michael said, building on Chase's misdirection. "Timmy thinks the only letters in team are *M* and *E*."

Michael had returned to Indigo Springs earlier in the summer for Johnny's wedding and stayed, recently becoming partners in his old friend's construction business. The more Chase got to know Michael, the better he liked him. That didn't mean Chase wouldn't give his new friend a hard time.

"Have you been hanging around my dad?" Chase

said with an exaggerated groan. "Because that is the caliber of bad jokes he tells."

Michael winced and covered his heart. "You wound me."

Johnny and Penelope laughed, but Sara wasn't listening to their exchange. "Is he married?"

"Of course Timmy's not married," Michael said. "He's eleven years old."

Sara rolled her eyes. "Not Timmy, his dad. Is Timmy's dad married?"

Chase had made it a point to find out Waverly's marital status about an hour ago. In doing so, he'd inadvertently learned that Waverly was quickly developing a reputation as a player.

"Divorced." Chase hoped that would end the line of conversation.

"I'm missing something," Penelope interjected. "Who is Kelly?"

Chase resigned himself to discussing Kelly. There was no way around it with this group. "She's in town looking for Mandy. And, as it turns out, she's helping me out with Toby. My dad was out of town last night so she babysat."

"Really?" Sara's eyebrows shot up. "Kelly Delaney babysat for you?"

Penelope lowered her voice. "If this Kelly Delaney is looking for Mandy, does that mean people know Mandy is gone?"

"More of them all the time," Chase acknowledged, a fact that made him uneasy. He'd allowed his father to convince him to delay going to DPW partly because they couldn't be sure Mandy had abandoned Toby, but he didn't honestly believe that. The more people suspected she wasn't coming back, the more Chase felt he should make that report to DPW. "It's not like it's a secret."

"Why is Kelly looking for her?" Penelope asked.

Sara exchanged a significant look with Chase. He'd already told her about Kelly retracting her story about the broken necklace, which had done little to curb her suspicions.

"Mandy owes Kelly money," Chase said.

Johnny whistled. "Must be a lot of money if she's going to this much trouble to find her."

Sara turned to Chase. "How much do you know about Kelly?"

Sara could just as easily have said once a liar, always a liar. Even though Chase at one time had believed that applied to Kelly, the heart-to-heart they'd had changed his mind.

"Enough to know she's a good person," Chase said. "But—"

"Sara," Michael interrupted, putting an arm around her and pulling her close. "What's with all the questions?"

Chase could have provided Michael with the answer. Sara had figured out he was attracted to Kelly and was attempting to look out for him. After the fiasco with Mandy, he didn't blame her for questioning his judgment when it came to women.

"I'm being a friend," Sara replied.

Michael kissed her on her temple. "Chase is a big boy. He can take care of himself."

"Of course he can," Sara said, "but what are friends for if not to butt into each other's business?"

Chase had to laugh. "I'm gonna remember that, Sara, but Michael's right. I can handle myself."

"But…" She didn't finish her thought, due to a gentle squeeze from Michael. She closed her eyes briefly, then said, "I'm sorry, Chase."

"Nothing to be sorry about. We all need somebody who's got our back." Chase winked at her and plastered on a smile. "If you'll excuse me, I'm taking Toby home."

"You're not staying for the fireworks?" Penelope gasped as though he'd announced he was leaving the country instead of the festival. "They're supposed to be spectacular."

"The little guy needs his sleep." Chase indicated the baby, whose eyes had once again popped open. He looked ready to break into full cry. "He's having a hard time getting any shut-eye with the noise."

He said goodbye and picked up the carrier, threading his way through the people who'd settled on the lawn to listen to the concert. He was halfway to his destination when he noticed Louise Wiesneski approaching him from the opposite direction. Avoiding the librarian would have been impossible.

"Well, hello there, Chase," she said. "How are things going with Toby?"

"Great. We're headed out now so I can put him to bed." He hid a grimace, wishing he didn't feel as though he was auditioning for Guardian of the Year whenever he dealt with Louise.

"So his mother isn't back yet?"

Toby started to whimper, which normally wouldn't have been a welcome sound. "Sorry, but we've got to go."

Chase stepped around her and proceeded to the far side of the park, where Kelly still talked with Jim Waverly. He felt as if he'd avoided one obstacle only to smash into another. They were deep in conversation with Waverly's blond head angled toward Kelly's dark one. She looked beautiful and feminine in a pale yellow cotton sundress, the skirt flowing around her slim legs.

"Let's focus on you," he overheard Waverly rasp in a low, deep voice as he approached. "When should we get together for that drink?"

Chase told himself he'd never been prone to jealousy, but the reminder didn't help as he waited for her answer. Kelly didn't give one. She spotted him and instantly put space between herself and Waverly.

"Chase!" Her voice sounded bright. Too bright. "Do you know Jim Waverly?"

"You're Timmy's dad, right?" Chase held out a hand, disguising the fact that he didn't feel friendly toward the other man. "Your boy's a heck of an athlete."

"Thanks." Waverly gave him a limp handshake without making eye contact, dropping his hand almost immediately. He muttered an insincere-sounding, "Good to meet you."

After an awkward silence, Chase said to Kelly, "I'm taking Toby home. If you're not ready to leave, my dad can give you a ride back to the house."

"Charlie said he didn't feel like staying for the fireworks," Kelly said. "I was just about to hunt for you so I could let you know he already left."

"I'll give you a ride home," Waverly offered as though it was already a done deal. He edged closer to Kelly. "That way you won't miss the fireworks."

"That's really nice of you, Jim." Kelly sounded as if she really believed Waverly had offered her a ride out of the goodness of his heart. "But I know you want to spend some time with your son, so I'll leave with Chase."

Was she trying to distance herself from Waverly or was that wishful thinking on Chase's part? He was still trying to figure out which as they headed down a side street where he'd managed to find a parking spot.

He debated whether to tell her about Waverly's reputation as a player. He didn't feel comfortable repeating hearsay, especially when he couldn't be sure it was true, but neither was he okay with saying nothing.

"You might want to be careful around Waverly," he finally ventured.

"What do you mean?"

He should have known she wouldn't accept his statement at face value. He shifted Toby's carrier from one hand to the other. The baby was sound asleep.

"Just be careful," he said.

"You know then?"

He stopped walking and regarded her curiously. "Know what?"

She pressed her lips together, obviously regretting her question. Her shoulders rose and fell as though now she was the one with the internal debate raging.

"What is it?" he prompted. "Is this about Waverly's reputation?"

She bit her lip, swiped a hand over her mouth and

nodded. "When you warned me about him, I assumed you knew he'd had an affair with Mandy."

Chase stared wordlessly at her, putting together pieces from the past. He remembered how heavily Mandy had relied on his father for babysitting. It seemed she hadn't spent all her time reading popular magazines at the library and sitting on a bar stool at the Blue Haven. She'd whiled away some of it in Jim Waverly's bed.

He waited for the sting of betrayal, but it didn't come. He'd felt markedly worse when he believed Kelly was falling for Waverly's act.

Chase placed a hand on Kelly's back. "Come on. Let's get out of here. We need to talk."

He had a destination in mind, and it wasn't the house to which his father had already retreated. He didn't care if Mandy had fallen for Waverly. But he did care, very much, what Kelly had discovered.

CHAPTER NINE

EVEN WITH DARKNESS muting the lushness of summer
and blurring the edges of the buildings, there was
enough of a moon to hint that the scenic overlook would
show off Indigo Springs to spectacular advantage at a
different time of day.

Kelly's impression that the town had a fairy-tale setting hadn't changed, but it was a place like any other.
Its beauty couldn't shield its residents from pain and
disappointment.

Chase hadn't said much since she'd broken the news
that Mandy had been cheating on him other than to suggest they not go straight back to the house. He'd driven
to the overlook, pulling into a small, empty parking lot.
Toby was fast asleep in the backseat.

She assumed Chase needed time to deal with the
knowledge of Mandy's affair. She crossed her arms over
her chest, wishing Chase hadn't been hurt by Mandy's
betrayal. He'd claimed not to be in love with her, but did
a part of him still belong to her? After all, she'd been
pregnant with his child.

"You're not cold, are you?" he asked.

The front windows of the Jeep were open, letting in

a cross breeze, but it was still close to seventy degrees. Realizing she'd been rubbing her arms, she immediately put her hands in her lap.

"Not cold," she said. "Worried about you."

"About me? Why?"

While she formed her thoughts, she leaned back against the headrest. The night was quiet except for the song of the crickets and the sound of the wind rustling the leaves of the trees.

"My ex-boyfriend cheated on me," she said without looking at him. It was easier to tell the story that way. "He's a teacher at my school. I found out at the movie theater when I was watching *Stepbrothers*."

"Isn't that a Will Ferrell movie?"

"It is," she said. "I'm a fan of his and I really wanted to see the movie. Vince—that's his name—kept coming up with reasons not to go. I finally went alone, and there was Vince a few rows in front of me, making out with another woman."

"That must've hurt," he said.

"Not for long." She made herself laugh. "I mean, come on, what self-respecting grown man has a make-out session at a Will Ferrell movie?"

"You've got a point."

"In retrospect, it was lucky I was there. Otherwise I'd probably still be with him."

"So you loved him?"

"Oh, no." She shook her head. "I loved the idea of him. He comes from this close-knit family and he seemed stable and dependable. I told you how I grew up. I guess I thought I could make a home with him."

"Why are you telling me this?" he asked.

Somewhere an owl hooted, leaves rustled and some twigs snapped. The nocturnal animals were waking up. She turned to look at him, determined he understand her point. "To let you know it's perfectly natural to be hurt."

"You think I'm hurt because Mandy was having an affair?"

She tried to make out his features in the darkness with limited success. "Aren't you?"

"I feel stupid for not realizing what was going on, but that's all. Things were pretty well over between us before they really got started."

She couldn't quite make herself believe him. She gestured to the overlook with a sweep of her hand. "If you didn't need time to compose yourself, what are we doing here? Why didn't we just go back to your house?"

"Because it's more private here," he said, "and I'd love to know if Jim Waverly has any idea where Mandy is."

She sat silent, stunned his reason hadn't occurred to her, not entirely sure why it hadn't. He'd explained the nature of his relationship with Mandy, yet she'd leapt to all the wrong conclusions.

"Well?" Chase prodded. "Did Waverly know anything?"

"He said Mandy told him her real last name wasn't Smith."

He seemed taken aback. "Any idea why she'd lie about her name?"

Kelly tried not to think about her own alias or the uncomfortable feeling that she was turning into the woman she was hunting.

"Waverly said he didn't know why," she said. "When he asked her about it, she clammed up, but she did tell him her name."

"Please tell me it's something unusual like Zanaletto or Yankovic."

"It's Johnson. Or so she told Jim Waverly."

"That figures," Chase said. "It won't be any easier to find information on a Mandy Johnson than it is a Mandy Smith."

"Yeah," Kelly said. "It seems like we can't catch a break."

"I take it Waverly doesn't know where Mandy went?"

"He says no," she said. "He also says she hasn't contacted him. He claims he didn't even know she planned to leave town."

"Do you believe him?"

She shrugged. "He doesn't have any reason to lie, especially after he admitted to the affair."

Headlights announced the arrival of another car, which pulled into the small lot and took the space farthest from them. A reason for the company occurred to Kelly.

"Can you see the fireworks from up here?"

"Only parts of them," Chase said, even as Kelly glimpsed an explosion of red, white and blue through the trees.

Nobody got out of the other car, further confusing Kelly. The view from their parking spot was even more obstructed than the one from Chase's Jeep. Kelly squinted, barely making out what looked to be a teenage girl in the passenger seat. The girl's head moved, away from the window, toward the driver.

Kelly let out a short, amused breath as the pieces clicked together. "Chase Bradford, is this where teenagers come to park?"

"Sure is." He reached across the seat, smoothing her hair back from her face. "Why do you think I brought you here?"

She felt her lips curve into a smile, the disappointment over the lack of progress in the search for Mandy temporarily forgotten. "To talk."

"Well, there's that," he said. "But can you blame a guy for having an ulterior motive?"

She realized she couldn't, not when she'd spent an inordinate amount of time thinking about kissing that guy again. Heat spread through her, the same way it had last night.

Not more than a few hours ago, she'd chastised herself for letting thoughts of Chase distract her from looking for Mandy. But it was late and there was nothing else she could do tonight to further her goal.

There wasn't much she could do to resist Chase, either.

"The only way I'd blame you is if you let a perfectly good parking spot go to waste." She tried to make her voice light but it came out husky with need.

He laughed anyway, meeting her halfway over the center console. His arms reached for her, his mouth fusing with hers. The passion was instantaneous as though they'd taken up at the exact moment their kiss had been interrupted the night before.

She'd never get tired of kissing him, she thought as he slanted his mouth to deepen the kiss. His hair felt thick and soft beneath her fingers, and he smelled warm and wonderfully masculine. She detected a hint of whipped cream and thought of what a good sport he'd been at the pie-eating contest, of what a good father he was, of what a good man.

She twined her arms around his neck, longing to be closer to him. She couldn't remember any other kiss or any other man, because this kiss and this man transcended them all. If only...

He pulled his mouth from hers, crying out in pain. "Ow."

She blinked, frustration warring with confusion. Confusion won. Had she bitten his lip? Pulled his hair? Poked his eye? "What's wrong?"

"The gear shift." The wince in his voice was audible. "It just got me."

"Where? In the leg?"

"No," he said. "It was, uh, another one of my appendages."

His meaning dawned on her. A giggle escaped, quickly transforming into a full-bodied laugh.

"You think that's funny, do you?" he asked.

"Sure do," she choked out. "I always heard it was dangerous to let a guy take you parking. I never realized until now *how* dangerous."

"Very funny," he said, but now he was laughing, too.

"I thought so."

"Too bad Toby's in the backseat," he said, "or I'd try to talk you into crawling back there with me."

He was joking. Chase Bradford wouldn't make love to a woman for the first time in the rear seat of a car. She knew that but put space between them anyway, straightening her sundress, smoothing her hair and hiding her frustration.

"It's probably a good thing he's back there," she said, "because I'm not the kind of woman who makes love and runs."

A pause, then, "Where would you be running to?"

She almost said New York, but then realized that would be a lie. "I think I should leave Indigo Springs."

"What!" He angled his body toward hers and ran a hand through his short hair. "You said you didn't have to be home anytime soon, right?"

"Well, yeah."

"So stay a few days. Wait to see if Helene Heffinger calls. What would it hurt?"

Part of the sky lit up in a blue flash, the color of the fireworks mirroring Kelly's mood. It made more sense to do as he said than to leave town, especially because the only place she could think to search for Mandy was Harrisburg, where Chase and Mandy had first met, but he had already looked there.

Kelly had gotten the message very clearly tonight, however, that her continued presence in town could hurt Chase.

"People are talking about us," she said. "That's why I stayed away from you at the festival. You still have Toby so they don't know Mandy left you. Some of them probably think you're cheating on her."

"I know that's not true and so do you," he argued.

"What about DPW?"

"What about it?" he asked.

"Aren't you afraid somebody will go to DPW and report that Mandy left you with a baby?"

"I can't see that happening," he said, "but it's a moot point. I plan to do that myself if I don't find her soon."

The set of his mouth told Kelly he'd made up his mind on the subject and there was no use arguing with him, no matter how skewed his reasoning.

"There's no sense in giving your neighbors room to gossip," she said. "At the very least, I should check into a hotel."

"It's the Fourth of July weekend. Rooms are scarce."

"You're telling me," she said. "I called around earlier today and couldn't find a vacancy until Tuesday."

Tuesday, just three days from now—and three days before her preliminary hearing.

"Then stay with us until Tuesday."

"Why?" Her eyes had adjusted to the darkness in the Jeep. He was leaning slightly forward, his features pinched. "Why do you want me to stay so badly?"

He didn't say anything for a long time. "Damned if I know. I just know that I do."

She was just as certain that she didn't want to leave. Not yet. The reason, she acknowledged, was only partly because she had nowhere else to go and could see what she could find on a Mandy Johnson. She was becoming far too attached to Chase Bradford and his baby boy.

"Okay," she said softly, the one answer her heart wanted to give.

As she uttered the agreement, she knew she couldn't stay in Indigo Springs indefinitely. If she didn't show up for her preliminary hearing on Friday, Chase would be unwittingly aiding and abetting a fugitive. Unless they came up with some leads soon, she had to think of Chase and leave.

CHAPTER TEN

"YOUR HEART'S FINE," Dr. Ryan Whitmore told Charlie at the conclusion of his Monday-morning appointment, wheeling back his chair and making some notations in a chart. "You'll be fine, too, as long as you stay away from spicy foods."

Charlie felt so weak with relief at the doctor's pronouncement he doubted his legs would carry him off the examining table and out the door.

He'd kept up an act all day Sunday, which he'd spent around the house with Kelly and Toby while Chase put in a very long day of work. He'd told Kelly so many of his jokes, he'd nearly exhausted his repertoire.

"I knew it all along." Charlie stalled for time to regain his equilibrium. "But wouldn't you know it? The bachelor doctor is the first one to believe me."

"Bachelor doctor?" The young man looked up from the chart, discontent marring his handsome features. Charlie had heard Dr. Whitmore had been a three-sport athlete in high school and he still had the body to prove it. "Where'd you hear that?"

"About a dozen places. So many I was hoping for advice on how to handle the ladies."

"Then you've come to the wrong place," he doctor said. "I haven't had a relationship that's lasted more than two months since high school."

"Sounds like you let someone get away," Charlie quipped.

"You can't lose someone you never had," the doctor said, a wistful look touching his face. "But don't ask me for advice. I can't even handle it when my own sister lays a guilt trip on me. How do you think she got me to fill in for her?"

"Good for her," Charlie said. "If you can't take advantage of a family member, who can you take advantage of?"

Charlie left the examination room with the doctor's soft chuckles sounding behind him, his legs having stopped trembling enough for him to check out at the reception desk.

"Heard you gave everyone quite a scare, Mr. Bradford." Missy Cromartie, the ultrayoung receptionist, handed Charlie his receipt. "You stay out of the emergency room, you hear."

"I only went because I heard they had some good-looking nurses, but not one was as pretty as you." He winked at her. "So I'm giving up the place."

Missy smiled, twin dimples appearing in her cheeks. "You stay out of our office, too. We don't want to see you until next year at your physical."

"As much as I like looking at your face, Missy, I'm in favor of that." He gave her a mock salute, then surveyed the empty waiting room. That was strange. Chase had driven him to his appointment so that Kelly would have a car since she was watching Toby, then insisted upon waiting. So where was he?

Charlie turned back to Missy. "Do you know where my son is?"

Her hands flew to her face. "Oh, yes, I forgot. He had some sort of work problem to deal with. I was supposed to tell you Mrs. Jessup will be here any minute to take you home."

Teresa?

Charlie had barely processed the thought when Teresa entered the waiting room, dressed in another one of her summery business suits. Only someone who knew her well would be able to tell she wasn't as cool and collected as she looked.

"Hello, be—" He remembered in time that he couldn't announce in public how beautiful he found her. "I mean, Te-resa."

She hurried over to him, placing a hand on his arm, appearing not even to notice his verbal slip. "What did the doctor say?"

She was worried, he realized. Really worried even though he'd reassured her days ago that the appointment was nothing more than a precaution. The spat they'd had at the restaurant dimmed to nothing.

He held his hands out at his sides, showman style. "The doc says I'm fine, the perfect specimen of health. How's your granddaughter?"

"She's fine, too," Teresa said. "Thankfully it was just a bump and not a concussion. But she's so little, I can understand why Andrea panicked and called me."

Andrea, the younger of Teresa's two adult daughters,

had two daughters of her own, both of them under three. Her husband, a pilot for American Airlines, was frequently out of town.

"Good thing she has you to call," Charlie said. "I can't think of a better person to turn to."

Missy got Teresa's attention to tell her the blood work from her recent physical had come back and everything was fine. The interruption reminded Charlie their conversation wasn't private. He waited while Teresa got a printout of her lab results, absurdly glad she wasn't angry with him anymore.

After they were in her car and she asked if he minded if she stopped by her house to let out the dog, his spirits rose even higher. They had to drive by her place en route to his, but he preferred to think that Teresa wanted to prolong their time together before she drove him home.

"Fine by me," he said. "Kelly's with Toby."

"That's what Chase said." She drove as competently as she did everything else, her slim hands at the recommended position on the steering wheel, her eyes on the road. "How much longer will she be in town?"

"At least for a few more days."

"I think Chase likes her," Teresa said.

"I think it's more than that," Charlie said. His son had been working around the clock since the festival, but Charlie had seen the two of them together enough to notice the attraction between them. "Hell, we're all a little in love with her. Even Toby. We'll be sad to see her go."

It didn't take Teresa long to reach the spacious four-bedroom house where she'd raised her family and now lived alone. The interior was spotless but welcoming, the warm colors of the furniture and the walls creating a homey feel.

"Thanks for coming to the doctor's office to get me, by the way," Charlie said when they were standing on her back porch, waiting for her dog to do his business.

"You're welcome." She quirked an eyebrow. "But I couldn't exactly say no when Chase called."

"You didn't want to say no," he said confidently. "I saw how worried you were at the doctor's office."

She watched the dog instead of him. "You're an old friend. Of course I don't want anything less for you than perfect health."

She walked closer to the edge of the porch, calling out, "Come here, Sweet Thing."

It was a silly name for a dog, especially one that might do well in an ugly-dog competition. Part pug and part something else, Sweet Thing had a compact body and a wrinkled face complete with a short, squat nose.

The dog waddled up the steps, its tongue lolling and tail wagging. Teresa crouched down and petted the dog, cooing, "You're a good girl, Sweet Thing. Yes, you are."

Just like that, Charlie was transported ten years into the past. He vividly remembered Teresa flinging open the door, her red dress slightly soiled, her face flushed, her arms full of a funny-looking dog he'd never seen before.

"Do you remember how Sweet Thing got her name?" Charlie asked.

Teresa looked up, the present colliding with the past. "Of course I do. Bill and I had you and Emily over for dinner that night. That was the night I finally admitted I had a pet."

"That's what happens when you keep feeding a stray."

"She knew she was mine before I did." Teresa scratched the dog behind her ear. "You and Emily sure were surprised when I answered the door, holding a dog."

"Only because—no offense meant, Sweet Thing— she'll never be offered a canine modeling contract."

"Emily was way more cool about it than you. She fell in love with her right away. Remember what she said?"

Charlie nodded, then they both said in unison, "Where'd you find that sweet thing?"

The two of them smiled at the shared memory, and in that moment Charlie felt as close to Teresa as he ever had. Then she broke eye contact, went into the house and the moment was gone.

"Charlie, would you lock the sliding door for me?" She'd adopted a brisk tone. His guess was that she was trying to reestablish distance between them, and he couldn't let that happen.

He put the security bar in place and locked the door, then trailed her into the kitchen, where he planned to suggest she put on a pot of coffee so he could linger for a while.

On the table was a community phone book opened to the Realtor section of the yellow pages. Red marker ink circled a display ad listing a popular real estate firm.

The breath left his body, freezing his limbs. He was jumping to conclusions. Even if Teresa was selling her house, it didn't necessarily mean she was leaving Indigo Springs. She could be downsizing. A four-bedroom house was far too large for one person.

He made himself breathe again, determined to ask Teresa about the phone book in a calm, rational manner.

She'd left her purse and keys on the kitchen counter. She picked them up, slung the purse strap over her shoulder and turned around. Her gaze ping-ponged from Charlie to the phone book and back again.

"I wasn't ready for you to see that," she said.

A chill settled over him. "Then you *are* selling your house?"

"I'm thinking about it." She inhaled as if the next words were hard for her to say. "Andrea wants me to move to Philadelphia to be closer to her and the kids. It makes sense. If I sell the house, I'll be able to retire."

He felt like he'd been broadsided by a linebacker. "But what about us?"

Her expression looked unutterably sad. "There is no us anymore, Charlie."

"How can you say that?"

"Because I couldn't tell Chase we'd been seeing each other when he asked if I knew where you were spending your time."

He tensed. Neither one of them had brought up Chase the other times they'd discussed the secrecy surrounding their relationship.

"He's the main reason you don't want anyone to see us together, right?" Teresa asked.

"Yes." Charlie was relieved to have it out in the open finally. "You know what Chase is like. You know how much he loved his mother."

Teresa nodded. "I know."

"Then you understand why I can't tell him?"

"I do," she said. "So I expect you to understand why I'm considering moving. I'm too old to sneak around, Charlie. Maybe it's time we both accepted that a romance between us isn't meant to be."

"But we won't have to sneak around forever," he argued, "just until more time passes."

"How much time? Three months? Nine months? A year?"

"I don't know," Charlie said helplessly.

"I know you don't."

They stood facing each other, barely three feet apart, but it felt as if an invisible wall was between them, signaling that they'd reached an impasse.

"We'd better go," Teresa said.

Charlie nodded and accompanied her in silence to the car while he tried to think of an argument that would get her to reconsider moving.

During the drive back to his house, though, for once he could think of absolutely nothing else to say.

ONE YEAR IN PRISON. Eighteen months probation. Psychological counseling.

Kelly disconnected her cell phone, the message Spencer Yates had left on her home answering machine still ringing in her ears. She hadn't checked her messages in days, irrationally afraid Yates had somehow figured out she was missing and had violated attorney-client privilege by reporting her to the police.

But as Saturday night blended into Sunday and then Monday with no word from Helene Heffinger, Kelly thought it best she know where her case stood.

Yates might not know she'd left town, but he had sounded mightily annoyed that she hadn't returned any of his phone calls. He demanded that she call him at once to talk about the plea bargain he'd worked out.

Good news, he'd called it.

"I managed to convince the DA you took the baby because you're having trouble dealing with your infertility," Yates said. "Luckily for you, he went for it."

That's where the counseling came in. Both her lawyer and the DA obviously thought she had a mental problem and couldn't be trusted around children.

Her prospects of ever being hired to teach again, already dim, grew bleaker.

She gasped aloud as something else occurred to her.

Because of her infertility, she'd always assumed she'd adopt a child someday. With a conviction and her questionable mental health as black marks against her, what reputable agency would approve her to be an adoptive mother?

"Kelly!"

Charlie's voice penetrated the closed door of the second-floor bedroom where Kelly had retreated to make her phone call. She got unsteadily to her feet, put her cell phone back inside her purse and opened the door.

Chase had left at dawn to patrol his territory for illegal hunting and fishing activity, and she and Charlie were alone in the house with Toby. Charlie didn't sound particularly distressed, but he could need her.

"Kelly!" Charlie called again when she reached the top of the stairs.

She cleared the thickness from her throat.

"I'm coming, Charlie," she called.

He appeared at the bottom of the steps before she completed her descent. "Oh, good. There you are," he said.

"What do you need?"

"A loaf of bread and some gravy mix. I put on that roast for dinner before I checked if we had everything." Charlie had started defrosting the roast yesterday, claiming it was coming to the end of its freezer life.

It was the kind of easily solved problem that popped up in the course of a day. In a microcosm, it represented the reason Kelly found living with the Bradfords so alluring.

Life here was just so darn normal.

For a woman facing a prison sentence that would strip her of her career and possibly the chance to be a mother, normal was intoxicating.

"I'd be happy to go to the grocery store for you," Kelly offered.

"I'd rather you keep an eye on Toby and the roast, if that's okay. He's in the family room."

It was more than okay, she thought a few minutes later while she was sitting cross-legged on the floor next to Toby and his building blocks.

She loved spending time with him. The only thing better would be if Chase could join them.

His work schedule had been so full they'd barely spent any time together since the fireworks display Saturday night, but she liked what she had seen of him.

Singing off-key in a duet with a character on *Sesame Street* with Toby in his arms.

Insisting he be the one who changed Toby's diaper before he rushed off to work this morning.

Leaving them both with a kiss.

"There's another block over there," she told Toby, pointing to a bright-red one under a Queen Anne armchair.

Toby crawled over to the block on chubby knees. He was such a champion crawler that she thought it was why he hadn't yet taken his first step.

She'd miss his first step, she realized. His first step and his first sentence and his first night in a big-boy bed.

She wasn't making any headway finding Mandy while sitting in the Bradford family room, no matter how attached she was getting to the trio of males who shared it with her.

A few days ago she'd decided against taking a trip to Harrisburg because Chase had already covered that ground. With her options running low, it was time to reconsider. She could recanvas the bar where he'd met Mandy and the hotel where the other woman had lived in case he'd missed something. This time she could ask if the name Mandy *Johnson* was familiar.

Toby suddenly started to whimper.

"What's wrong, Toby?" she asked, gathering the little boy into her arms.

He screwed up his face, in obvious discomfort. He felt a little warm even though Charlie had lowered the setting on the air conditioner to counteract the heat from the oven.

Ten minutes later, Toby was wailing as she walked him around the house. She'd also identified the source of his distress—he was teething.

"I'll get something to make it better, sweetheart," she told him.

She found baby aspirin and gel to rub on his sore gums, but neither of them helped. Then she remembered a tactic to get him to calm down that Chase had shared.

"C'mon, little guy," she said, heading for the door. "We're going outside."

CHASE LEFT HIS JEEP in the driveway, even though he could see through the row of small windows lining the top of the panel door that the one-car garage was empty of his father's car.

He'd spent the day like a nomad, constantly on the move as he patrolled his territory for illegal fishing activity, but his mind kept returning to one place.

Home.

Even though he hadn't grown up there, he'd started thinking of the Cape Cod on Elm Street as home almost as soon as his parents had relocated. His mother's death had rendered the place merely a house, but the people who filled it were slowly transforming it into a home once again.

His father, whose health had checked out just fine at the doctor's office to Chase's tremendous relief.

Toby, whom he loved without reservation.

And Kelly, who...well, he wasn't ready to put a label on what he felt for her.

He'd been so busy at work both today and yesterday that they hadn't made any progress in their search for Mandy. They needed to put their heads together and come up with a firm plan.

Not tonight, though. Tonight he planned to enjoy the company of his three favorite people. He walked quickly toward the house, then stopped suddenly. A dull, steady noise rang in his ears.

Trying to identify the source, he surveyed the immediate vicinity. But no, the noise wasn't coming from outside. It was emanating from…the house?

He hurried toward the entrance, the noise growing incrementally louder with each step he took. He tried the doorknob, found it unlocked and yanked open the door.

A shrill mechanical scream assaulted his ears. The smoke alarm!

At the end of the short hallway that led to the kitchen, a haze of smoke wafted in the air.

Oh, God, no!

Heart pounding and adrenaline surging, he raced toward the kitchen.

"Kelly!" he screamed. "Toby!"

He braced himself to get assaulted with a wall of heat, dreading the sight of flames licking at the walls, of Toby and Kelly unresponsive on the floor.

But he saw no fire, only smoke.

It curled toward the ceiling in thin gray puffs, its origin the oven. His eyes stinging from the smoke, he hurried over and turned it off. He pulled on the thick oven mitt beside the sink, then yanked open the oven door and hauled out a shallow pan. Inside was a beef roast, overcooked but not burned, swimming in bubbling juices.

He put the pan on the counter and bent down, finally identifying the cause of the smoke. The juices had spilled over the side of the pan and splashed on the heating element.

Luckily it wasn't true that where there was smoke, there was fire.

He drew in a relieved breath, the smoke immediately clogging his lungs and making him cough.

He flicked the switch that turned on the oven fan, then located the still-shrieking smoke alarm, jerking out the batteries.

Returning to the kitchen, he spotted an unopened package of baby spinach beside an empty salad bowl. Kelly had obviously been in the middle of preparing dinner, but then where was she?

"Kelly!" he called, his voice less frantic.

She didn't answer, which seemed strange. Where would she have gone when there was a roast in the oven, especially since his father seemed to have taken the car?

His mind still on the puzzle, he moved to open the kitchen window that overlooked the backyard. There, dashing through the sprinkler that was set to switch on automatically in the early evening, was Kelly. She held Toby securely in her arms.

He opened the window, barely noticing the clean, sweet air that streamed into the house, his attention focused on the woman and the baby.

They were a good distance away, which was probably why she hadn't heard the alarm. Chase saw the white flash of her teeth. He could tell Toby was also smiling by the way the little boy waved his arms. They were both drenched.

Amid the smoke and the smell of overdone beef,

something inside him softened, radiating from his heart until his chest felt full.

He finished opening the rest of the windows on the first floor, enabling a cross breeze to flow through the house. Then he went into the backyard, still transfixed by the sight of woman and baby.

Kelly was making another pass under the sprinkler, singing loudly and off tune about raindrops falling on their heads. Toby's giggles were so infectious Chase felt his lips curve upward. Kelly looked up, a broader smile wreathing her face.

"Look, Toby," she said. "Look who it is."

Toby stopped giggling. Stretching out his arms, his mouth still open in a charming grin, he said, "Da-da."

Time seemed to freeze.

Chase noticed little things. The drops of water in Toby's hair. Kelly's slim, sure hands at the baby's waist as she half lifted him toward Chase. The happy sparkle in Toby's eyes.

The moment burned into his memory as surely as if he'd taken a photograph, Chase reached for the little boy he thought of as his son.

Toby came willingly, flapping his arms with delight as though he were still playing in the sprinkler.

"Da-da," he said again.

Chase's throat felt thick, rendering him momentarily speechless.

"That's the first time he's called you that," Kelly stated.

Chase cleared the thickness from his throat. "You can tell, huh?"

"Oh, yeah."

"How you doin' today, sport?" he asked Toby, although the answer seemed fairly obvious. Chase would be doing great, too, if he'd spent the day with Kelly.

The little boy patted his own head.

"He's telling you the raindrops were falling on his head," Kelly translated.

"Yeah, I saw that," Chase said.

"I wanted to take his mind off his t-e-e-t-h." Kelly spelled out the last word. "More of them must be coming in because he was crying something awful."

"We have some gel in the medicine cabinet that's supposed to help," Chase said.

"He was already in full cry when I tried that so I brought him outside to distract him. The sprinkler came on, and the next thing I knew we were running through it." Kelly pushed her wet hair back from her face as she relayed the story. Her T-shirt clung to her curves very nicely. "It seemed to work."

"How long ago was that?" Chase asked.

"Maybe a half hour. Not long after your father went to the grocery store. I told him…" Her voice trailed off and she smacked her head. "The pot roast! I told him I'd watch the pot roast but I totally forgot."

She hurried toward the house, with Chase following. "Kelly! Wait! There's something you should know before you go into the house."

She turned around, her expression pained. "I ruined it, didn't I?"

"Almost, but that's not it. Some juices got on the heating element so the house is pretty smoky."

She cradled her head with both hands. "I'm so sorry.

I shouldn't have left the house with something in the oven. I don't know what I was thinking."

"I do." He closed the distance between them. "You were thinking of a way to get Toby to stop crying, and you did that."

"Yes, but—"

"No buts." Balancing Toby with one arm, he reached out with the other and covered her lips with two of his fingers. "The house is smoky, but so what. There's no harm done."

"Yeah, but no self-respecting cook would have let that happen. I guess the secret's out that I'm terrible in the kitchen."

"You're wonderful with Toby, and that's far more important." Chase lifted the boy in the air, relishing his immediate baby giggles. "Isn't that right, Toby? Isn't Kelly the best?"

They waited a few more minutes for the smoke to clear, then went into the house, working in tandem to rescue the edible parts of the roast.

The rest of the evening didn't play out exactly as Chase had envisioned, but it was close enough. His father was strangely subdued during dinner, something so out of character that Chase did something he'd sworn he'd never do.

"You're actually suggesting we play charades?" Charlie asked. His father paid little mind to the fact that it was a party game, better played with a group of people. Whenever they had a guest in the house, even it if was only a single guest, Charlie tried to get up a game.

Chase always resisted, partly because the game was

corny but mostly because his father was a spectacularly lousy player.

"Yeah," Chase said. "But if you make a big deal of it, I might change my mind."

At the threat, his father leaped to his feet. As always, he insisted on going first. Ten long minutes later, he collapsed against the sofa cushions.

"How could you guess *Babe* when the answer was *King Kong?*" his father asked Kelly, his voice laced with mock exasperation.

"They're both movie titles," Kelly said, giggling. Toby, who was sitting on her lap, giggled, too.

"Yeah, but King Kong's a big ape," his father said, sounding put out. "Babe is a little pig."

"You indicated it was something fat."

"Not fat. Big. An ape can be big and not be fat. A pig is always fat. There's a real distinction. How could you get them mixed up?"

Kelly's giggles turned to full-fledged laughter, and she wiped at her eyes. Chase smiled, enjoying the affectionate interplay between the two. Kelly belonged here, just like his father, just like Toby. She'd told him earlier that she loved Indigo Springs. Maybe he could persuade her to stay.

"Look at it from my standpoint," Kelly said. "You described an ape the same way you would a pig."

The phone rang, interrupting their mock argument. Chase was closest so he rose from his seat beside Kelly and picked up the portable receiver on the third ring. "Hello?"

"This is Helene Heffinger." The jewelry-maker's

voice came over the line, so unexpected it was jarring. He covered the mouthpiece, walking quickly out of the living room and away from the noise. "It turns out I did have that phone number you wanted."

A sense of foreboding swept over him, although he wasn't sure why. "Do you have a name?"

"Of course I have a name," she said testily. "I wouldn't have the phone number if I didn't have a name, too."

"What is it?" Chase prodded.

"Jasper Johnson."

Johnson. The same last name that allegedly belonged to Mandy.

While Heffinger gave him the rest of the information, Chase watched his father, Kelly and Toby, all of whom where still laughing. For them, nothing had changed.

But in the space of a phone call, Chase's entire world had been upended.

Mandy had always maintained she didn't know who had fathered Toby. She also claimed she'd never been married. Those statements could still be true but it struck Chase as too big a coincidence that Mandy shared a last name with the man who'd bought her the necklace.

On the day Toby had called him Da-da for the first time, Helene Heffinger might have just provided Chase with information that could lead him to the baby's biological father.

CHAPTER ELEVEN

GO-KARTS WHIZZED AROUND a serpentine track Tuesday night, mostly driven by male teens too young to hold drivers' licenses.

Kelly spotted only one couple in line, the female half of the pair a petite blonde who was dwarfed by her tall, brawny boyfriend. They held hands, their eyes mostly on each other rather than the noisy machines circling the track.

If she tried hard enough, Kelly supposed she could pretend she and Chase had driven an hour to the Allentown track known as Scooters in search of a fun, unusual date. But she was too old for fairy tales, even though she'd been living one for the past few days in the company of the Bradford men.

She'd made a step in the right direction this morning by moving out of Chase's house and back into the Blue Stream Bed-and-Breakfast. Now it was time to bring her search for Mandy back to the forefront, where it belonged. She was running out of time and money. No matter what happened tonight, she needed to stop fooling herself that she and Chase were a normal couple.

She needed to harden herself against falling in love with him.

"Are you sure we're in the right place?" she asked him.

They were standing outside a chain-link fence that looked over the track, just steps from the small building where customers paid admission and teenagers played video games.

"Pretty sure," he said. "I kept getting the answering machine when I called the number Heffinger gave me, but Scooters is definitely the right place. Heffinger remembered that Jasper Johnson worked as a go-kart attendant."

"That doesn't mean he still works here," she said.

"True, but it's time we caught a break."

He took a few deep breaths as though he was steeling himself, too, but she knew his private battle had everything to do with Toby. "Are you ready to do this?"

She put a hand on his arm to detain him. "You know, Jasper Johnson may not be Toby's father."

Chase had put forth his suspicion about Toby's parentage when he'd gotten off the phone last night, but since then had shied away from discussing the issue. His sigh was audible even over the track noise. "I guess it's pretty obvious I've been worried about that."

"I've become attuned to the Bradford men over the past few days," she said. "When something's bothering you, you clam up. Your dad jokes around."

"My dad always jokes around," he remarked.

"Not so much now that he and Teresa are having trouble."

"What do you mean having trouble?"

"They're involved, aren't they?"

"What!" His mouth gaped open, and he shook his head. "My dad and Teresa aren't involved."

"Are you sure?" She'd gotten the opposite impression at the festival, when Charlie had been overly interested in Teresa's whereabouts. Just yesterday Charlie had told her Teresa was considering moving to Philadelphia. He'd claimed to be concerned that she'd be making a mistake but Kelly thought he was more worried about losing her.

"Of course I'm sure," Chase said. "They've been friends for years but that's it. Besides, my mother hasn't even been gone a year."

Kelly didn't believe love followed a timetable, but now wasn't the time to discuss it, especially with Chase so uneasy over the prospect of meeting Jasper Johnson.

"Then I must be wrong." She put her hand over his and squeezed, disguising her own nervousness. With her preliminary hearing fast approaching, she had as much at stake as Chase did. "Ready?"

Inside the building the teenage boy behind the ticket counter directed them outside to the track. "Yeah, J.J.'s here. Ask around. He won't be hard to find."

On the track a small contingent of men wearing red Scooters T-shirts shuffled young thrill seekers in and out of go-karts, making sure their seat belts were secure, then helping them unstrap. The most impressive employee was a muscular fair-haired man in his twenties who resembled Jim Waverly, but about twenty percent inflated.

"I think that big guy over there might be him." Chase spoke into her ear, the apprehension in his voice hinting he'd also noticed the man's resemblance to Waverly. It followed that a woman who'd been involved with Waverly would also find the muscular, blond Scooters' employee attractive.

"Hell, no. I'm not Jasper Johnson." The blond snorted when they finally got his attention. He spoke in a loud voice to be heard above the roar of the go-karts. "J.J.'s over there with the tattoos."

The man he indicated was a wiry five foot six or seven, with thick forearms decorated with what looked like tattoos of eagles. He had a receding hairline and appeared to be in his late forties or early fifties, easily twice Mandy's age. He said something to one of his co-workers, then skirted the line of chatty teenagers, disappearing around the side of the building that housed the video games.

Chase thanked the muscular blond, then took Kelly's hand. "Let's go."

She had to hurry to keep pace with him as they followed the path the man had just taken. She shared his urgency. Although the go-kart complex was entirely fenced, she was irrationally afraid Jasper Johnson would disappear.

Instead he was leaning against the side of the building, one leg bent at the knee and braced against the concrete, smoking a cigarette. He regarded their approach warily.

"Are you Jasper Johnson?" Chase asked. The building blocked some of the noise, making it possible to talk without shouting.

The man grimaced. "Aw, hell. I only missed the one time."

"Missed what?" Chase asked.

"The probation meeting." Jasper Johnson's already small eyes narrowed. He did not look friendly. "You're a cop, aren't you? Because you sure look like a cop."

Chase didn't deny what was essentially the truth. "I'm here as a friend of Mandy's."

Johnson straightened from the wall, his posture tense. "Where is she?"

"We were hoping you could tell us," Chase said. "We're looking for her."

"And you think I know?" Johnson made a disbelieving sound, then resumed his position against the building and took a long drag of his cigarette before answering. "Hell, I haven't seen her since I got out of the joint. Must've been a year and a half ago."

That was the same time frame Heffinger had given. Kelly quickly did the math. Toby was a year old, which meant that eighteen months ago Mandy would have been three months pregnant. If Johnson's estimate was correct, he couldn't possibly be Toby's father.

She produced Mandy's broken necklace and showed it to him. "Is that when you gave her this?"

His tough-guy expression faltered before he quickly resurrected it. "She said she was going to keep that. Did she give it to you?"

"No. She lost it. Why? Does it have special meaning? Is that why you had it made for her?"

"How'd you know I got it made for her?" he demanded, his face turning red. "Did she tell you I ripped her last one off her neck? 'Cause that's not true. It was an accident!"

The quick flare of Johnson's temper hinted otherwise. Kelly took a step closer to Chase before offering an explanation. "Helene Heffinger told us about the necklace. That's how we found you. She said you showed her a drawing and commissioned her to reproduce it."

"So what? A father's got the right to give his daughter a necklace."

"You're her father?" Chase sounded stunned.

"She told you I was dead, didn't she?" Jasper Johnson's voice was harsh. He nodded at Chase. "You her boyfriend?"

"Ex," Chase said. "Have you been in touch with her lately? Maybe have a phone number for her?"

Johnson took another drag of the cigarette, the smoke filling the air between them. "I've been trying to find her myself. We're having a bit of a…misunderstanding."

"What kind of misunderstanding?" Kelly asked, but figured it had something to do with the necklace he'd ripped off Mandy's throat.

"She didn't accept my apology, okay?" Johnson threw the cigarette butt on the ground and stomped it out with his foot. "Why all the questions? Why you looking for her? What's she done?"

Chase didn't hesitate. "She ran out on me."

"You and me both, man." He walked back toward the go-kart track, not even bothering to say goodbye, smoke lingering behind him.

"Did you get the feeling Jasper Johnson is the reason Mandy was going by the name of Smith?" Chase asked.

"Most definitely," Kelly said. "I wouldn't be surprised if he was in jail on an assault charge."

"If that's true," Chase said, "Mandy should have told me about him."

"Maybe she was embarrassed," Kelly said. "It's not always easy to tell someone you have a parent in prison."

He gazed steadily back at her, realizing instantly what she'd admitted. "Your father?"

"I lost track of him a long time ago, but no..." She'd been so young all she remembered about him was her mother's assertion that he wasn't interested in being a father. "I was talking about my mother."

"She's the reason you went into foster care when you were only eight," he said, a statement not a question.

If he'd asked what crime her mother had committed to land her in prison, Kelly might have skirted the question. Because he'd focused on the lost little girl she'd been, she found herself wanting to tell him everything.

"She stabbed another woman to death. They were at a party and they'd been drinking pretty heavily. She claimed self-defense, but witnesses said they'd been arguing. Over a man, I think, although that was never clear." She took a breath, determined to finish the story. "She got thirty years to life. It might have been less but she had a rap sheet. Shoplifting, DUI, drunk and disorderly. That kind of thing."

Motors hummed and teenagers shouted, but she barely noticed the background noise. Her focal point was his face. She waited, barely breathing, for him to regard her differently, the way most people did when they found out about her mother.

He took hold of her hand, a simple gesture but one that spoke volumes. He squeezed gently, offering her his support. "Do you keep in contact with her?"

"I visit her once a year on her birthday, but that's it," she said, finding it easier to tell the rest of it. "I was never a priority in her life so I can't let her become one in mine. Being related by blood isn't enough. Some people just aren't cut out to be parents."

"Like Jasper Johnson?" he asked.

"Yes," she agreed. "And Mandy. I've spent only a few days around you and Toby but I can already tell the best place for him is with you."

She couldn't gauge what impact her reasoning was having on him, but needed to make him understand. She took a step closer to him, wanting to make sure he heard her above the hum of the nearby go-karts. "That's why you can't go to DPW. Even if there's only a chance they'll take Toby away from you, you can't risk it. You have to keep him with you."

"I know," he said.

His statement represented such a huge departure from his previous position that she needed to make sure she'd heard him correctly. "You know? When did this happen?"

"Just now. When we met Jasper Johnson."

"So let me get this straight. You no longer feel like it's your duty to report to DPW that Mandy abandoned her child?" she asked.

"That's right," he said, quite an admission from a man who usually viewed the world through lenses that filtered every color except white and black. "My duty to Toby is more important."

"Is that why you didn't tell Johnson he had a grand-son?"

"That's why," Chase said, steel in his voice. "This doesn't mean I'm going to stop looking for Mandy. I'm not. If I don't find her in another week or so, I'll hire a P.I. I have time."

He was right. Now that he'd let go of his stubborn insistence to do things by the book, Toby could stay exactly where he was. Chase did have time.

But for Kelly, time had run out.

"Now I have a very important question to ask you," Chase said, his countenance grave.

She peered at him, hoping it wouldn't be a question she couldn't answer truthfully.

His expression suddenly cleared, his eyebrows dancing. "Wanna race me? I'm hell in a go-kart."

The conclusion he'd come to regarding Toby had lightened his mood, but Kelly's heart was heavy because she'd made a decision of her own. She smiled at him anyway, determined to enjoy what was left of the evening.

"You're on," she said.

A short time later as they raced their go-karts around the course and through the winding turns, they took their eyes off the track at regular intervals to grin at each other. The wind whipped through Kelly's hair, along with the certainty that she'd come to the right conclusion.

She'd yet to decide whether to return to Wenona for her preliminary hearing, but every day that passed brought her closer to being a fugitive.

With that prospect looming over her, she couldn't in good conscience continue to keep company with the law-enforcement officer who had found his way into her heart.

Chase might have altered his stance on reporting Mandy's abandonment to DPW, but the essence of who he was hadn't changed.

That's why she needed to leave Indigo Springs.

Tomorrow.

CHAPTER TWELVE

THE HOMEMADE BLUEBERRY scones at the Blue Stream Bed-and-Breakfast were so renowned that rumors abounded of townspeople booking a room just to experience the breakfast that came with it.

The last time Kelly had stayed at the B and B, she'd arrived for breakfast so late in the morning that all the scones were gone. She'd made sure that didn't happen today, showing up in the quaint Victorian-style room where breakfast was served in plenty of time to nab one of the rich, savory pastries.

She transferred the scone to a piece of flowery china, poured herself a cup of fragrant coffee and sat down at an empty table. Then she picked at the treat, unable to judge its merits because her taste buds were as numb as her heart.

She glanced at the clock on the wall, surprised to see that ten minutes had gone by since she sat down. Ten minutes that took her closer to leaving Indigo Springs.

She could only afford to linger a little while longer over breakfast before it would be time to gather her meager belongings and set off for the bus station. Her destination was Harrisburg, the city where Mandy had been living when she met Chase. It was the only place Kelly could think of that might yield clues to Mandy's whereabouts.

Kelly didn't fool herself that Mandy was in Pennsylvania's capital, waiting to be found. She'd dismissed the idea earlier, but with the hearing only two days away she had no recourse but to cover the same tracks Chase had. She planned to question people who'd known Mandy, hoping Chase had missed something the first time around.

She'd be forced to use some of her finite supply of cash to rent a car and check into a hotel. She didn't want to think what would happen when she ran out of money—or if she didn't find evidence to exonerate her.

"There she is, Toby. There's Kelly."

Wondering if she was hearing things, her head jerked up at the familiar voice. But there was no mistaking the baby's sweet face or the gray-haired man holding him. Charlie waved, then strode to her table.

"Good morning, Kelly," he said, as though meeting over scones at the Blue Stream B and B was a regular occurrence.

"'Morning, Charlie."

Toby held out his arms, effectively conveying his meaning. Kelly took him from Charlie, gathering him close and breathing in the scent of baby shampoo. She had no trouble interpreting the nonsense words he was babbling.

"I'm glad to see you, too, Toby." She looked over his head to Charlie. "What are you two doing here?"

"We came to have breakfast with our favorite girl,

didn't we, bud?" Charlie chucked Toby lightly under the chin. "After Chase left for work this morning, Toby went room to room searching for something. I finally realized it was you. So here we are."

The anecdote touched her. In the time she'd spent with Toby, she'd learned she didn't have to be related to a child to love him.

Charlie placed a small container of dry cereal and a bottle of juice in front of Toby, then told Kelly, "Be right back."

The little boy picked up some of the *O*-shaped cereal but not with his usual gusto. He sniffled and laid his head against her chest, his small body warm against hers. She kissed his soft hair, trying not to think this would probably be the last time she held him.

Charlie returned to the table shortly, a steaming cup of coffee in one hand and a plate containing a blueberry scone in the other.

"I thought only guests got scones." Kelly expected him to make a joke, perhaps along the lines of the owner not being able to resist him, possibly even suggesting she'd propose if she wasn't already married.

"The owner's father is a friend of mine," he said.

Kelly blinked, a bit taken aback by the very un-Charlie like answer, then asked, "Have you had the scones before?"

"I love them," he said. But his pastry, like Kelly's, sat untouched on his plate. Toby, too, ignored his cereal.

"Is Toby all right?" she asked.

"I'm not sure," Charlie said. "I'm afraid he might be coming down with something. What do you think?"

She laid a hand on his forehead, which felt cool to the touch. "He doesn't have a fever but he seems listless. It's probably just a little cold, but you should keep an eye on him."

Charlie nodded.

"How are *you?*" she asked.

"Fine," he said quickly. Too quickly.

"Really?" she ventured. "Because it seems to me that's something's wrong."

"Wrong? What could be wrong?"

"I don't know, but you're not your usual cheerful self." She laid a hand on his arm. "It's okay if you don't want to talk about it, but I'm a good listener."

He closed his eyes briefly, seeming to debate her offer. When he spoke, it was clear the words didn't come easily.

"We drove past Teresa's house on the way here. There's a for sale sign in her yard." Charlie rubbed his forehead as though his head hurt. "I knew she was thinking about selling, but I didn't think she'd go through with it."

"Is she planning to leave town?"

"Her daughter wants her to move to Philadelphia."

"And you want her to stay in Indigo Springs," Kelly finished.

He nodded miserably, confirming what Kelly had suspected all along. Something was going on between Charlie and Teresa.

"Then tell her you love her," she advised.

He almost knocked over his coffee, managing to right the mug at the last moment. "How do you know I love her?"

"Because of the way you look when you talk about her," she said. "But some women need to have it spelled out. Teresa might be one of them."

"Teresa already knows I love her." He lapsed into silence, staring down at his hands, then mumbled. "That's not why we're having problems."

"Then what is the problem?" Kelly asked gently.

He raised his head, and for the first time since she'd met him she noticed the wrinkles on his face. "The worst time of my life was when my wife died. Teresa was greatly affected, too. They were closer than sisters. But she hasn't even been gone a year. How would it look if I took up with her best friend?"

"Who cares how it looks?" she retorted.

"I care," he said. "How could Teresa and I be truly happy if our being together hurt other people?"

"Who would it hurt?" Kelly tried to make sense of his rationale and arrived at the only possible conclusion. "Are you talking about Chase?"

The way his eyes flicked away from hers told her she'd guessed right. Charlie rubbed a hand over his jaw. "He loved his mother.

"He loves Teresa, too," Kelly said.

"That's not the point. You've gotten to know him. Do you really think he'd approve of me being in love with another woman only nine months after his mother died?"

"You don't know for sure that he'd disapprove," she said, even though she'd seen his shocked reaction to the possibility the other day. But Chase had altered his position on DPW and Toby. Maybe he wasn't quite so hard-line as they all believed. Maybe she could talk to Chase and make him understand that love was precious, no matter where—or when—you found it.

"I can see in your face that you want to help, but you can't," Charlie said. "I told you about Teresa in confidence. I need you to promise you won't mention it to Chase."

His comment brought the truth crashing down on her. How had she forgotten, even for a second, that she wouldn't be around to persuade Chase of anything?

"You don't have to worry, Charlie." She briefly debated telling him she was leaving town, then decided not to. She couldn't risk Chase finding out and trying to persuade her to stay. Besides, she'd never been great at goodbyes. "I won't tell him."

Toby rubbed at his eyes and whimpered. She bounced him on her knee, staving off a cry, but the tactic wouldn't work for long. She smoothed his fine hair and kissed his soft cheek, feeling her own tears prick the backs of her eyes.

"It looks like Toby's already ready for his nap," she remarked.

"He got up at the crack of dawn this morning," Charlie said, "probably because he wasn't feeling well."

"Then he needs his rest. You should take him home."

Charlie nodded and stood, reaching for Toby. Kelly's arms clung to the boy for long moments before she finally surrendered him. She stood up, too, noticing neither she nor Charlie had come close to finishing the scones that were supposed to be so delicious.

"I wish you hadn't moved back to the B and B," he said.

Kelly didn't know how to reply to that without revealing she was leaving for good, so she said nothing. She'd given both Charlie and Chase the impression she planned to stay in Indigo Springs for a few more days, continuing to search for clues on Mandy's whereabouts. Clues she now accepted she wouldn't find.

"You're perfect for him, you know," he said.

She swallowed, aware that wasn't true.

Kelly Delaney, the uncomplicated elementary-school teacher who'd grown up in a two-parent family and had never been in trouble in her life, was perfect for Chase.

Kelly Carmichael, whose mother was in prison and who might soon end up there herself, wasn't.

"You're perfect for Teresa." She stood on tiptoe and kissed him on the cheek. "I hope you two work it out."

"Me, too," he said but didn't sound hopeful.

She watched until Charlie and Toby were completely out of sight before heading back to her room, stuffing her belongings into her backpack and checking out of the B and B.

She tried not to think about all she was leaving behind as she walked the few blocks down Main Street to the bus stop, but the tactic didn't work. Her mind kept drifting to how things might have been had she met Chase under different circumstances.

Would they hold hands when they walked side by side, the same way as the couple coming toward her on the sidewalk? Envy gripped her and unshed tears blurred her eyes. She blinked a few times, clearing her eyes of moisture, just as the couple drew even with her.

The woman, who was about twenty years older than

Kelly but in fantastic shape, wore a T-shirt depicting an image of a happy turtle. A familiar image.

"Wait!" Kelly cried, startling both of them. She stepped in front of the couple, forcing them to stop, aware from the looks on their faces that they thought she was crazy. "I'm sorry. But could you tell me where you got that T-shirt?"

The man backed up a step, taking the woman with him. His wary gaze shifted from Kelly to the giant tongue on his shirt. He was older than he'd first appeared, gray hairs visible in the dark hair he wore in a ponytail. "At a Rolling Stones concert."

"Not the tongue." Kelly gestured to the woman's shirt. It was pink, the same color as the one she'd found rolled up under the bed in Mandy's room. "Where did you get the happy-turtle shirt?"

The woman's grip on the man's hand was tight enough to stop circulation. Kelly tried smiling to put her at ease, but Kelly's anxiety quotient was so high the smile probably looked feral.

"It's not a happy turtle," the woman finally said. "It's a dancing turtle. They sell them at the restaurant."

"What restaurant?" Kelly asked.

"The Dancing Turtle. It's in Fox Tail, a little town in the Poconos near the New York border. It's kind of a tourist trap but I thought the shirt was cute."

"It is cute. Very cute. Thank you so much," Kelly said, probably overenthusiastically. The couple edged away from her. "I'm sorry for stopping you. Thanks again."

Both their heads bobbed, then they quickly crossed the street.

Kelly glanced at her watch, then walked briskly in the opposite direction of the bus stop, the trip to Harrisburg forgotten. The public library opened in fifteen minutes, and she planned to be first in line to sign up for a computer with Internet access to find out all she could about the Dancing Turtle.

An hour later, after making a long-distance call to a place called Fox Tail, Kelly was on the phone, looking for Chase. She got his voice mail. "This is Chase Bradford. Leave a message at the tone."

"Chase, this is Kelly. Call me as soon as you get this." She didn't attempt to keep the excitement from her voice. "I've found Mandy."

FOG ROLLED OVER THE mountain, hugging the four-lane highway that cut a swath through the Poconos. Chase eased his foot off the gas pedal and kept his eyes on the slick road. He didn't even dare glance at Kelly, who was in the passenger seat.

He'd phoned her at the bed-and-breakfast immediately after getting her surprising message about Mandy, but they'd decided to wait until after he finished work to set out for Fox Tail.

The little town in the northern Poconos was less than two hours from Indigo Springs, and the restaurant where Mandy worked included a bar that stayed open until 2:00 a.m.

"I hope the woman I spoke to on the phone doesn't tell Mandy somebody called asking about her," Kelly sounded worried.

"Did you tell her not to?"

"It seemed smarter not to say anything. I thought she'd tell Mandy for sure if I made a big deal out of it."

The day had been hot and sticky until a recent rain shower had cooled the air, the perfect conditions for fog, which was thicker up ahead, making it feel as if they were driving through a cloud. Chase slowed down another ten miles per hour.

"I just hope she doesn't run," Kelly said.

"Why would she?" He drove through the thickening murk, his attention divided between his driving and the conversation. "All I want from her is permission to raise Toby, and she probably thinks she got away with stealing your money."

"Neither of us knows very much about her," Kelly mumbled. "She could be guilty of other things, too."

The faint glow of red taillights suddenly appeared out of the misty whiteness, signaling a car ahead of them. His heart hammering, Chase swerved the Jeep into the passing lane, traveled a safe distance in front of the car and switched back into his original lane. Then he slowed down yet another ten miles per hour.

"The fog's getting heavier," Chase said. "We may have to stop."

"We have to keep going," Kelly protested. "Mandy's working tonight."

"I didn't even see that car we just passed until we were almost upon it," Chase said. "In a few miles we have to leave the highway and take the back roads. Visibility will be even worse."

"I'm willing to risk it," Kelly said.

Headlights suddenly appeared in the rearview mirror,

followed by the blare of a horn. The headlights, attached to a blue sedan going much too fast, veered into the passing lane. A pain radiated down Chase's spine, no doubt because he was holding his body so rigidly. He gripped the steering wheel so hard his short fingernails dug into his palms.

"I'm not willing to risk your safety," he said. "I can't see the signs, but I'm pretty sure there's a hotel off the next exit. I'm going to stop."

"But Mandy—"

"Will probably be working tomorrow, too," Chase interrupted firmly. "We can't keep going, Kelly. It's not safe."

"Then shouldn't we turn around and head back?"

"That would be almost as dangerous," Chase said. "The fog probably won't lift until morning. We have to spend the night in a hotel."

The exit was only about another mile, but it felt like an eternity before they reached it. Visibility was so poor that Chase almost missed the exit ramp, even though he was looking for it. He took the S-curve slowly and carefully, but one of the front wheels still ran onto the shoulder before he righted the Jeep.

He'd never been happier to see a hotel. The establishment was exactly where he thought it would be, the upper two stories rising out of the fog. A bored-looking clerk was on duty, the paperback mystery novel he'd been reading open on its spine. He straightened when they approached the desk. "Fog chase you in?"

"It's as bad as I've seen it," Chase said. "There aren't many people on the highway."

The clerk nodded and punched in a few keys on the computer. "All our rooms are nonsmoking. You'd like a single, right?"

Kelly glanced at him, a question in her eyes. He'd been so concerned with the fog and his disappointment in not being able to settle things with Mandy tonight that he hadn't thought ahead to their sleeping arrangements. His heartbeat sped up. He nodded.

"Right. A single," Kelly told the clerk.

"Is a king-size bed okay?" the clerk asked.

Chase squashed his inclination to tell that clerk that hell, yeah, they wanted the king-size bed. The decision was up to Kelly.

"Two double beds would be better," she said.

His heartbeat slowed back down and disappointment cut through him. He should have known the meaningful glance she'd slanted him had to do with whether they should share a room, not a bed.

"It seemed wasteful to pay for two rooms," she said as they walked down the hall in the direction the clerk had pointed.

He unlocked the door with the key card and pushed it open, revealing a standard hotel room with two beds, a desk and chair, a television and a small bathroom. The color scheme consisted mainly of creams and light oranges, the decorations bland enough to offend no one.

The door closed behind them with an audible thunk and all Chase could think about was tumbling onto one of the beds with her. That wouldn't do.

He raised his eyebrows, the way he'd seen his father

do a hundred times, his intention to cut the tension. "You can trust me not to take advantage of you, but can I trust *you?*"

She stared at him mutely, her lips slightly parted, her breathing not as steady as it had been a moment ago. The tip of her tongue appeared, moistening her lips. His silly throwaway line, it seemed, had had the opposite effect of what he'd intended.

He felt his groin tighten, but he didn't move. Not his hands. Not his feet. Not even his lips.

It struck him that they were alone, with neither his father nor Toby acting as unsuspecting chaperones. Alone in a hotel room with two beds, only one of which they needed to use.

Mere moments ago he'd told her she could trust him. He couldn't touch her, not without an invitation.

"I think…" she said slowly, the huskiness of her voice fueling his hope "…we should go get a drink."

"A drink?" he repeated dumbly, hoping he'd heard her wrong.

"A drink." She was already moving toward the door, talking as she went, sending disappointment cascading through him. "There's a bar off the lobby."

Even though she hadn't touched him, he was in no condition to be seen in public. Not yet.

"You go ahead," he said, then came up with a legitimate excuse for him to hang back. "I need to call my dad and let him know about the fog."

She was sitting at a table for two when he arrived, the bar nearly deserted except for the bartender and one other couple.

"I ordered you a draft beer," she said, not quite meeting his eyes. "I hope that's all right."

"It's perfect." He picked up the mug and took a healthy swig.

"Is everything all right at home?" She was sipping from a glass of white wine, which caused Chase to focus on her lips. He almost groaned.

"Toby's still not quite himself," he said. "My dad thought he felt a little warm and gave him some Tylenol. I'll call tomorrow morning and check on him again."

He took another swig of beer. He'd never done any acting, but thought he deserved an Oscar for not showing his frustration. "How about you? Are you feeling any better?"

"Better?" She looked puzzled. "I'm not sick."

"You *are* nervous."

She winced, looking charmingly embarrassed. "Is it that obvious?"

"Oh, no." He shook his head in an exaggerated motion. "You seemed perfectly poised when you sprinted out of the hotel room."

She laughed. "I was not sprinting."

"Okay. Jogging, then."

"It was your fault! You're the one who made the suggestive remark."

He leaned closer to her and said in a quiet voice, "I suggested you might have trouble keeping *your* hands off *me*."

"Yeah," she said. "Like the trouble I had the night your father was out of town and I couldn't sleep. And again when we went to that lookout during the Fourth of July festival."

"I remember not being able to keep my hands off *you* those nights."

"Okay, then," she said. "Since we've established we both have trouble keeping our hands off each other, that's even more reason to be nervous."

"But why?" he asked. "Is it that jerk who cheated on you? Is that why?"

"Partly." She picked up her wineglass. "I didn't tell you the whole story about him."

"Then tell me now."

She took a long sip of wine, then another before she spoke. "After I've been out with a guy a few times, but before it gets serious, I make it a point to tell him it's unlikely I'll ever have children."

She took a deep breath as though filling herself with courage instead of air. "I have something called premature ovarian failure, which basically means my ovaries don't produce enough hormones for me to ovulate regularly. I've known about it since I was seventeen. It's ironic really, considering I became a teacher because of how much I love kids."

"You can love kids that aren't your own."

"I know that," she said. "But when I told Vince I'd need fertility treatments if I ever wanted to get pregnant and chances were even that wouldn't work, I could tell it bothered him."

"After you told him, is that when you saw him at the movie theater with the other woman?"

"That's when," she said. "I broke up with him, but it was pretty obvious he was relieved. I'm sure he wants to have biological children one day."

"Not all men think like that," he said. "I couldn't love Toby more if he was my own."

"But you also would have married a woman you didn't love because she was having your baby."

"Apples and oranges," he said. "Toby's as much my responsibility as a biological baby would have been."

"Admirable," Kelly said.

"Or stupid, considering Mandy was never pregnant." Chase blurted out the secret he'd never told anyone. "That miscarriage? She faked it, the same way she faked the pregnancy."

"She didn't!" Kelly seemed appalled.

"She did," Chase said. "I confronted her a couple of days before she left town. She'd been drinking or she probably wouldn't have admitted it."

"Wow," Kelly said. "I had no idea."

"Neither does anyone else. I felt like such a sap I didn't tell anyone. Not even my father."

"A sap?" She shook her head vigorously. "I might not always agree with you, but you can't be a sap for sticking to your principles and doing what you think is right."

"I don't know about that," he said, "but all I have to do is look at Toby and I'm not sorry things happened exactly the way they did."

She reached across the table, covering his hand with hers and looking deeply into his eyes. The mood between them shifted, the air becoming more charged.

"Chase?" she said softly. The candlelight on the table cast her face in a soft, beautiful glow.

"Yeah?" His response was equally soft.

"I'm not nervous anymore."

THE HOTEL-ROOM DOOR wouldn't budge.

Kelly stood alongside Chase, their bodies touching, watching the red light flash. They hadn't lost physical contact since they'd left their unfinished drinks on the table in the bar and hurried down the hall, desperate for privacy.

"Damn." Frustration laced Chase's soft curse. Kelly's body trembled with the same emotion.

He shoved the key card in the slot again. The small dot turned red. Again.

"Let me try." Kelly rasped.

She took the card from him, flipped it around and attempted to gain entry. That darned little red beacon flickered again.

"I don't know what's wrong," Kelly said.

"The door must be stuck." Chase gave the unyielding rectangle a hip bump. The resulting thud echoed down the hallway.

The door swung open, the space in front of them filling with a heavyset man in a T-shirt and Bugs Bunny boxer shorts. The man's face reddened and his scowl deepened.

"Who the hell are you?" he bellowed. "And why are you trying to get inside my room?"

His room?

Kelly checked the numbers painted on the door. One twelve, not one twenty-one.

She sucked in a breath through her teeth. "Sorry. Wrong room."

The man glowered, then slammed the door in their faces with so much force air whooshed over them. She and Chase exchanged a guilty look, then moved down the hall with alacrity to room one twenty-one. This time the key card worked perfectly.

As soon as they were inside the room, they burst out laughing.

"Did you see that Bugs Bunny underwear?" Chase asked, swinging her into his arms.

Kelly looped her arms around his neck and nodded. "They sure cut down on his intimidation factor."

"That's why it's better to wear nothing at all to sleep," Chase said, his lips at her neck.

Delicious shivers traveled the length of her body. "You think so?"

"I know so."

He found her mouth, kissing her with unrestrained enthusiasm, his hand traveling from her waist to her breast. She gasped at the sheer pleasure of being in his arms, stunned at how quickly they'd moved from laughter to passion.

She barely had the strength to draw back from his mouth so she could build upon his suggestion. "Chase," she whispered against his lips, "let's get naked."

She didn't have to ask twice. He tugged at his T-shirt, lifting it over his head. Her shirt and bra came next. They were standing at the foot of the bed nearest the door. They toppled onto the mattress, his lips on her bare breasts, her hands at the waistband of his pants.

The bed was so narrow, they nearly rolled off the edge.

"We should have gotten the king," he said.

"I don't know about that." She disentangled herself from him and sat up, wriggling out of her skirt and underwear. "The closer I can get to you, the better."

He swung his legs over the side of the bed and started taking his own clothes off so quickly it felt as if they were racing to see who finished first. It was a draw. As soon as they were naked, they turned to each other, their bodies and their mouths coming together with no hesitation. His bare skin felt warm and thrilling against hers.

She hadn't known it could be this way, she thought as he kissed her. He knew just where to touch her to get her to sigh, how to kiss her to beg him to go faster, when the moment was exactly right to join with her.

Their lovemaking was so effortless. So…right. When he entered her and they started to move together, what she felt was unmistakable.

It was joy.

CHAPTER THIRTEEN

WARMTH ENVELOPED KELLY, a growing awareness of the source pulling her out of a languorous sleep. A man's hand was splayed over her stomach, moving higher until it covered her bare breast.

She sighed with contentment, thinking it had been silly for her to worry last night that neither of them had clothes to sleep in.

They'd been much happier wearing nothing at all.

She turned her head and found his mouth, letting him kiss her awake, his tongue doing delicious things to hers. Sensation shimmered the length of her body, the hot spot at her very core.

She opened her eyes to find him looking at her. His lips clung to hers for a moment before he drew back.

"Good morning," she said.

"I'll say." He widened his eyes slightly, making her smile. "It was a good night, too."

For the rest of her life, Kelly would remember the details. The laughter after the man with the Bugs Bunny underwear had slammed the door in their faces. The passion when they were finally skin to skin. The elation when they made love.

She turned more fully into him, pushed the fingers of one hand into his hair and let her other hand roam from his shoulder on down, discovering he was already hard.

"We can make it an even better morning," she said.

"I'm up for that," he said.

She was still smiling when he kissed her. Last night blended with this morning so that they were nearly indistinguishable.

Every time is as good as the first time, she thought, when you're in love.

"Are you okay?"

He was poised above her, his eyes looking deeply into hers. She realized she'd gasped at the realization that she loved him. She should have figured out last night that she felt such joy because she was in love.

She loved him!

The thought was both wonderful and terrifying.

"Couldn't be better." She pulled him down to her and before long she could barely think at all.

A little while later, she lay next to him with his arms wrapped around her midsection, his lips against her hair. Now that her powers of reasoning had returned, she didn't want to think about the repercussions of being in love with him. Not when this moment—this man—was perfect.

She smiled. *Perfect.* That was the word Charlie had used about her and Chase.

"I need to call my dad," Chase said as though he sensed Kelly had been thinking of his father, too. "I want to see how Toby is."

Chase took his arm from around her and sat up in bed. He had the lean musculature of an outdoorsman. His chest was lightly sprinkled with hair, his abdomen flat. Kelly didn't think she'd ever seen a more appealing man.

"Try not to worry," Kelly said. "Toby's probably fussy because he's teething, but it wouldn't hurt to have Charlie take him to a pediatrician to check it out."

"The pediatrician is what I'm worried about."

"Why?"

"He doesn't have one. Not in Indigo Springs anyway."

"Then register him as a new patient."

He shoved a hand through his hair. "If he needs to go to the doctor, he'll go, but there will be questions. Mandy didn't leave any of his papers behind. Not his shot records. Not the name of the pediatrician she used in Harrisburg. Nothing. Hell, I don't even have his birth certificate."

Kelly sat up, too, struck by something he said. "You don't have Toby's birth certificate?"

"I don't have squat."

Kelly's stomach churned as a sick feeling came over her, but Chase wasn't looking at her. He was already swinging his long legs over the side of the bed and getting up.

"What time did you say the Dancing Turtle opens?" he asked, picking up his cell phone from the top of the desk.

It took her long moments to retrieve the information from her reeling brain. "Eleven o'clock."

"We need to get going. I'll tell my dad we won't be back until later this afternoon. We can have breakfast on the way to Fox Tail. Then, with any luck, we'll find Mandy."

Everything came back to Mandy, Kelly thought numbly.

"You can use the bathroom first," he said.

She got out of bed like an automaton, sensation returning, but only barely, when he waylaid her on the way to the bathroom to kiss her lingeringly on the lips. "Just so you know, I'd rather stay in bed with you."

When she was inside the bathroom, Kelly leaned back against the closed door.

Charlie had told her early on that Toby wasn't Chase's biological son, but it hadn't occurred to her until now that the little boy might not be Mandy's son, either.

Maybe the reason Mandy hadn't left behind Toby's birth certificate or medical records was because she didn't have them.

Mandy had kidnapped and abandoned one child. Who's to say she hadn't done it twice?

She closed her eyes as the dire realization that she and Chase were operating at cross purposes struck her.

If they found Mandy in Fox Tail, Kelly would have the ammunition she needed to get the police to look deeper into her case.

But if Toby was a kidnapped child, Chase could very well lose the boy he loved so dearly.

CHASE FINISHED OFF THE last of his three-egg omelet, washed it down with black coffee and sat back to regard Kelly.

She'd hardly said a word since they'd made love this morning. She'd eaten her food, but did so mainly in silence, listening as he outlined a strategy for when they reached the restaurant where Mandy worked.

"When we get there, I'll go in without you," he said.

"If she's there, she has no reason to avoid me. You'd have to think she plans to get in touch with me eventually about Toby."

"You'd think that," Kelly mumbled, which was about as verbal as she'd gotten this morning. He hadn't noticed how quiet she'd been until after they'd set out for Fox Tail and stopped along the way at this chain restaurant for breakfast.

"If she's not there, I'll ask to speak to the owner and tell him why I'm looking for her," Chase said. "With any luck, that should get me Mandy's home address."

This time Kelly's only response was a nod. Not for the first time that morning, Chase had the impression she wanted to tell him something. "Is everything okay?"

He'd thought she looked pale under her tan before he asked. Now her complexion bordered on white.

He swallowed, then said with difficulty, "If you're having second thoughts about making love to me—"

"I'm not having second thoughts," she interrupted.

"Thank the Lord."

She smiled, but only barely.

"Then are you feeling okay?" he asked.

"I'm fine," she said, unconvincingly. "But I do need to use the restroom."

She got up, grabbed her purse from the vacant chair beside her and hurried away from the table. He heard something clatter to the floor. A hairbrush. He leaned down to pick it up and noticed a lipstick and wallet had also fallen out of Kelly's purse.

He reached for the items, intending to place them on the table so she'd easily spot them when she returned.

Her wallet gaped open when he picked it up, revealing a plastic window containing a New York driver's license.

Kelly looked beautiful in the official photo, her hair thick and shiny, her lips curved into a smile. Chase smiled, too. He had it bad, he thought, if a driver's license photo could get that kind of reaction from him.

He was about to snap the wallet closed when he noticed the name beside the photo: Kelly Carmichael.

Carmichael, not Delaney.

He stared in shock, hardly able to process the information. But there was no mistaking what was in front of him.

The license belonged to a green-eyed, five-foot-seven-inch brunette from Wenona, New York.

Wenona, not Schenectady.

He made his reeling mind focus. Could the discrepancy be due to a simple change of address? No. He remembered Kelly saying she'd taught at the same school for several years, and Wenona and Schenectady were too far apart to commute. Besides, there was the matter of the different last names.

She'd lied to him.

He shouldn't be surprised.

It seemed forever ago since she'd arrived in town spouting the unbelievable tale of the broken necklace, but in reality it had only been a week.

A week in which he'd ignored all the warning signs.

A week in which he'd let his heart override his common sense.

He jotted down her driver's-license number on a napkin he then stuffed into his pocket, and numbly closed the wallet and placed it on the table along with the brush and the lipstick.

"Can I get anything else for you today, sir?" Their waitress approached the table, not realizing his world had just been turned upside down.

"Just the check," he said.

She tore a sheet off the pad and handed it to him. On the check, beside the amount, she'd drawn an incongruous happy face. He withdrew a few bills, adding a healthy tip.

"I think I love you," the waitress said, the word resonating inside him.

Kelly walked toward him from the direction of the restroom. Their lovemaking was so recent that he could still easily call to mind the way it felt to be inside her.

He desperately wanted to believe there was a sensible explanation for why she'd given him a false name and hometown.

She sat down at the table. Her face was still pale but looked damp as though she'd splashed water on it.

It took a supreme effort to sound casual. "Feeling better?"

"Yes, thank you."

A stiff formal answer, one she might give to a stranger.

"I've been thinking about something," he said slowly, not sure what he was going to say until it was out of his mouth. "Once this business with Mandy is over, maybe I could come up to Schenectady some time to visit."

Her eyes dipped to the table and she swallowed, her throat constricting. Maybe those weren't beads of water on her forehead, he thought. Maybe they were drops of sweat.

He waited, hardly knowing what for.

"I'd like that," she said softly.

He felt as though he'd been sucker-punched. He realized he'd been waiting for the truth, that he might have forgiven her anything if she'd only stop lying to him.

Her gaze returned to his face. Her smile looked tremulous. Fake. It didn't comfort him that she wasn't quite bold enough to meet his eyes because the harsh reality was that he'd been duped again.

Kelly's lies should probably seem minor in comparison to Mandy's whopper about being pregnant, but Kelly's deception was worse because he hadn't been in love with Mandy.

He rejected the word as soon as it came into his mind. He could never love a liar. He wouldn't let himself.

"Is something wrong, Chase?" Kelly asked.

Her words were similar to the ones he'd spoken to her before she headed off to the restroom.

They could have it out. Right here. Right now. But Chase had given her a chance to come clean when he'd made the remark about visiting her in Schenectady.

"I have a phone call I need to make," he told her. "I already paid the check, but you can wait for me in here where it's cool."

He didn't give her a chance to refuse, getting up and striding outside into the dawning heat. He walked around to the side of the restaurant where he'd have privacy and dialed his friend at the police department.

"Are you in the office?" he asked when Dave McPhearson picked up the phone. "Because I need you to do something for me."

"Good morning to you, too," Dave said.

Chase took a deep breath. "Sorry, buddy. This is important. I have another name I need you to check out, but this time I have the driver's-license number."

"That makes it a whole lot easier," Dave said. "Just let me get to a computer."

Chase heard the sound of footsteps, then some shuffling and clicking of computer keys.

"Let's have it," Dave said.

Chase recited the driver's-license number, then told him it belonged to Kelly Carmichael of Wenona, New York. He felt as though he was saying the name of a stranger.

He stayed on the line for what seemed like an hour but couldn't have been more than a few minutes.

"Got it," Dave said, then whistled. "This Kelly Carmichael is in hot water. She's out on bail but her preliminary hearing is tomorrow, then it looks like she'll be headed to prison."

When he got his voice to work, Chase asked, "What's the charge?"

"Kidnapping."

His heart felt as if it stopped before it resumed a slow, painful beating. He listened while Dave outlined the specifics of the case.

His mind rebelled that Kelly could be guilty of such a crime, but he reminded himself that his experience with Mandy had proven he wasn't the best judge of character.

Even if he took what Dave was telling him at face value, Chase couldn't come up with a connection between Kelly and Mandy.

From the first, that had been what bothered him. Why was Kelly so desperate to find Mandy?

Before he went inside the Dancing Turtle to confront Mandy, he intended to find out.

A HUGE STATUE OF A TURTLE, its legs protruding at absurd angles from an upright shell, marked the entrance to the Dancing Turtle.

The restaurant was on a stretch of road with a gas station and a country store but little else, but Kelly supposed isolation drew tourists to this part of the Poconos. Once the sun went down on the lakes and streams and hiking trails, the Dancing Turtle would present a viable option for whiling away the evening hours.

She and Chase had yet to get out of the Jeep, which was parked in the gravel lot facing the restaurant. Silence reigned between them. Since they'd stopped for breakfast, he'd acted like a stranger instead of the passionate man to whom she'd made love.

She attributed his mood to worry over Toby and the custody situation. His father had called that morning to say he thought Toby might have an ear infection, necessitating he make an appointment with the pediatrician.

If Toby was another kidnapped child, Chase had good cause for alarm.

The eggs and toast Kelly had eaten churned uneasily in her stomach. Could she really let Chase walk into that bar without knowing what Mandy had done and what it might mean to Toby?

"I need to tell you something," Kelly said.

She hugged herself, praying she'd have the strength

to get through with the confession. "My name isn't Kelly Delaney. It's Kelly Carmichael. Kelly Delaney is a woman I went to college with."

He said nothing, his expression unchanging, as though the information didn't even come as a surprise.

She took a ragged breath. "About a week and a half ago, I saw a woman at the playground near my house with a crying baby."

She could have been talking to a robot, so little emotion was on his face, but she kept on, telling him all of it. About the woman asking her to take care of the baby for just a few hours. About the cops coming to the door. The arrest. The eyewitness picking her out of a photo lineup.

"That woman at the park," Kelly said, "was Mandy."

He sat silently beside her, the seconds ticking interminably by until he finally asked, "So it's not true Mandy owes you money?"

"No," Kelly said. "I'm looking for her because the cops aren't. Once the eyewitness identified me, the police didn't believe me when I said someone else was the kidnapper."

His expression was so stoic she couldn't tell what he was thinking or whether he believed her.

"I'm sorry I lied to you, Chase, but you have to understand I couldn't afford to trust anyone." She swallowed. "Especially not somebody in law enforcement. I'm out on bail, but I wasn't supposed to leave New York."

"Why are you telling me this now?" he asked, his voice without expression.

They'd reached the most difficult part of her story, the one that would be hardest for him to accept.

"Because of something you said this morning about Toby." She fell silent, praying for the strength to continue.

"What does Toby have to do with this?"

She forced out her suspicion. "I'm afraid Mandy might have kidnapped Toby, too."

She expected shock or dismay, but he exhibited neither. "And how did you reach this conclusion?"

Her lips trembled. She bit the bottom one with her upper teeth to stop it, trying to gather herself. "You said you didn't have Toby's birth certificate. Or any identifying papers at all. Mandy could have kidnapped Toby before you met her."

He crossed his arms over his chest.

"You don't believe me," she stated.

His arms stayed crossed. "You don't exactly have a track record of telling the truth."

She'd been so worried about Toby that she hadn't considered how telling him the truth would impact her. The worst had happened. She'd put her heart on the line and he'd stomped on it.

"I'm telling the truth now." She reached into her purse and pulled out her wallet. "I can show you my driver's license."

"That's convenient."

"What do you mean?"

"Come off it, Kelly. You must know I've already seen it."

"What? How?" She thought back over the past few hours and remembered returning from the restroom to discover her wallet and some other items had fallen out of her purse. "Did you go through my wallet?"

"I picked up your wallet and it came open," he said.

"Did you have somebody run my driver's-license number?" she asked. "Was that why you needed to make a phone call after breakfast?"

"Yeah," he said. "That's why."

"Then you know I told the truth about who I am and the charges I'm facing." She could tell she'd hit a nerve.

He continued to stare at her, giving away nothing.

"I'm telling the truth, Chase. Don't you see what this means? Mandy kidnapped one baby that I know of. She could have done the same with Toby."

Some movement caught Kelly's eye and she noticed a woman wearing short shorts and a Dancing Turtle T-shirt walking on a path leading from a cabin in the back of the restaurant.

The woman's gait was instantly familiar. Kelly leaned forward, waiting for her to get closer so she could get a better look. The woman was neither a brunette nor a redhead. Her hair was cut short and bleached blonde, but there was no mistaking who she was.

"It's Mandy," Kelly said.

Mandy rounded the corner of the restaurant, walked past the ridiculous turtle statue and disappeared inside.

"Wait in the Jeep," Chase said. "Give me ten minutes and then come in after me."

He reached for the door handle, but she stopped him from getting out of the vehicle with a hand on his arm. She felt his muscles tense.

"I'm telling you the truth, Chase," Kelly said with as much conviction as she could muster.

"We'll find out soon enough," Chase said. "The answers are inside the bar."

CHASE TRIED TO FALL BACK on his law-enforcement training as he headed away from the parking lot. If he could stay detached, he had a better chance of sorting out what was truth and what was fiction.

His sweating palms and pounding heart told him he didn't have a chance of keeping his emotions uninvolved.

Too much was at stake.

The boy he loved as a son might belong to another family. A family that could be experiencing tremendous heartache and fear.

Stubbornly refusing to put a label on what he felt for Kelly, he continued on his path. He discovered upon entering the building that the Dancing Turtle was two establishments in one.

An entranceway with a wooden bench seat built into the wall and doors leading to his and her restrooms served as a bridge between two large rooms. On the right side was the bar, which seemed deserted. On the left a restaurant stood empty, aside from an elderly couple who sipped from glasses of water.

The rustic decor featured wooden booths and tables situated on a worn hardwood floor. Chase settled into a booth that had a view of the kitchen. He could hear people moving about and pots and pans clattering as the staff got ready for the lunch crowd.

Within minutes, Mandy emerged from the kitchen

carrying two cups of coffee. She wore black shorts and a snug-fitting pink T-shirt sporting the image of the dancing turtle. With her short, bleached blond hair, she was almost unrecognizable.

She set the coffee on the couple's table and took an order pad from the pocket of her shorts, focusing on the male of the pair. She leaned too close to him, touched him on the shoulder and laughed at something he said.

Chase knew now that the flirtatious act was Mandy's way of getting what she wanted, whether it be a big tip or a man who'd support her until she was ready to move on.

Mandy finished scribbling down the couple's orders and repocketed the pad, then seemed to notice for the first time that there was someone else in the restaurant. She headed toward him, her step faltering only slightly along the way. She didn't stop until she reached him. She even smiled, although there was a tightness around the edges of her mouth.

"Why, if it isn't Chase Bradford." She cocked a hip and placed a hand on the waistband of her shorts. "Isn't this a surprise."

"It shouldn't be," he said. "You must know I'd be looking for you."

"How did you find me?"

He gestured to her T-shirt. "You left one of those behind. The logo is pretty distinctive."

"So you missed me." She batted her eyelashes, the same way she had that night in Harrisburg exactly six months after his mother's death. But today he was no longer drunk or grieving.

"Drop the act, Mandy," he said. "I'm here because of Toby."

She instantly sobered. "Is he all right?"

"He's fine. Doing great, actually. No thanks to you."

Her lips thinned. Gone were both the flirtatious waitress and the concerned mother, replaced by the woman who'd manipulated him. "Are you trying to lay a guilt trip on me?"

"I'm trying to do what's best for Toby." He found he couldn't refer to Toby as her son, not until he checked out Kelly's claim.

"And you think I'm not?" Her voice rose at the end of the question, drawing the gazes of the elderly couple. She cleared her throat, then spoke in a lower, yet no more insulted, tone. "What kind of person do you think I am?"

"You don't want to know the answer to that." She looked around, determined nobody else was coming into the restaurant and slid into the booth across from him. "I left Toby with you because that was the best thing for him."

Chase regarded her, noticing her resemblance to Kelly, even understanding how an eyewitness could have gotten them mixed up.

"Don't you mean you did the best thing for you?" he asked.

"Yeah," she said roughly. "Maybe I do. What's so terrible about that?"

"A mother's supposed to put her baby's needs above her own."

"You don't think I know that?" Mandy hissed. "You

don't think it's been hell for me to admit I'm not cut out to be a mother?"

"I don't know, Mandy. After the way you played me, I don't know anything about you."

"I did what I had to do. I got Toby a good home," she bit out, then seemed to tense. "Unless you're here because you don't want him anymore."

"Of course I want him," Chase refuted. "I love him."

Her posture relaxed. "So what's the problem?"

"I don't have a legal leg to stand on. I'm not his father. I'm not even his guardian. DPW could take him away from me in a heartbeat."

"DPW?"

"The Department of Public Welfare," Chase said. "I want you to sign over custody. I want to adopt him."

He watched her carefully for a reaction. If she agreed, she'd have to provide Toby's birth certificate and Chase would have proof that the boy wasn't a kidnapping victim.

But if she didn't...

"Kelly!" Mandy was no longer looking at him, but at a point beyond his shoulder.

He didn't have to turn around to determine that Kelly had gotten tired of waiting in the Jeep.

"What are you doing here, girl?" Mandy was smiling so broadly nobody would have guessed she'd just been asked to give up her son.

Or that the woman at whom she was smiling had been charged with a crime she claimed Mandy had committed.

What the hell was going on?

KELLY HAD ENVISIONED COMING face-to-face with Mandy a hundred times since her arrest.

Not once had she anticipated Mandy smiling and greeting her by name.

But it was going to be all right. By calling her by name, Mandy had just admitted she knew her. Chase would have to believe Kelly now.

Keeping her composure, Kelly sat down in the booth next to Chase. She wet her lips and said, "I'm here because I was arrested for a crime you committed."

"Crime?" Mandy screwed up her features. "What you talking about, girl?"

Kelly's heart sank. Kidnapping was a felony. She should have known Mandy wouldn't own up to the crime, but she hadn't anticipated the other woman would act as though she was auditioning for a part in a play.

"The little boy you kidnapped in Utica and left with me," Kelly said. "You said his name was Corey, but it was really Eric."

"What?" Mandy laughed loudly enough that the elderly couple looked in their direction. "Are you playing with me? Is this some kind of joke? Because I don't know anything about a kidnapping."

Chase hadn't said anything during their exchange. Was he buying Mandy's act?

"She's lying, Chase," Kelly insisted. "You've got to believe me, please."

But why should he believe her? No matter Kelly's reasons, she'd done a lot of lying herself since she'd met him.

"You two know each other?" Mandy looked from

one of them to the other, a hand at her throat. "How did that happen?"

"I came to Indigo Springs, searching for you," Kelly said.

"Because you say I kidnapped some kid?"

"Because you *did* kidnap him."

"Oh, come on!" Mandy said. "Why would I leave my son behind and then go kidnap another kid? It makes no sense."

"Maybe you kidnapped Toby, too."

Mandy laughed harshly. "Why would I kidnap my own son?"

"Because he's not your son," Kelly ventured.

"You have a hell of a lot of nerve coming in here and making trouble for me." Mandy shook her head back and forth. "You were always a little off, but I never thought you were crazy."

"Why are you acting like we know each other?" Kelly asked.

"Because we do," Mandy said. "You teach elementary school in Wenona. At some private school."

"I told you that when we met in the park," Kelly said.

"What park? We met at the University of Buffalo."

"I told you that, too."

Mandy turned to Chase. "I didn't go to school at UB, but I had some friends who did. I used to run into Kelly at parties. People were always telling us how much we looked alike."

"That's not true!" Kelly cried.

Mandy fingered her short blond hair. "Not anymore it's not."

Kelly's brain raced, trying to come up with a strategy to get Mandy to incriminate herself but she could already feel the bars of the cell closing in on her.

"How long have you worked here?" Chase asked Mandy. A smart question. The kidnapping had occurred two weeks ago. If Mandy hadn't yet started at the Dancing Turtle, she would have had opportunity to kidnap the child.

Did that mean Chase was leaning toward believing Kelly, or was he merely asking the question any law-enforcement officer would?

"Three long weeks," Mandy said. "We're shorthanded so I haven't had a day off since I started. Good thing this job comes with a place to live or I'd have quit by now."

Kelly understood that Mandy was providing an alibi. If she'd been at the Dancing Turtle every day for the past three weeks, she couldn't have kidnapped a baby in a different state a week and a half ago. Except Kelly knew she had.

"Can anybody vouch for that?" Chase asked.

"My boss can." Mandy stood up. Was there a certain smugness in her attitude? "I'll go get her. I need to put in this order anyway."

"I'll come with you," Chase said. A smart move, Kelly thought. That way, he could make sure Mandy didn't ask her boss to lie for her or try to make a run for it.

Chase got out of the booth and followed Mandy into the kitchen, barely sparing Kelly a glance. She told herself his cool demeanor meant nothing, that he was trying to get to the bottom of a sticky situation, but her nerves were on edge.

If she couldn't get Chase to believe her, what chance

did she have of convincing anybody else that she'd been wrongly accused?

She expected to have to wait for a while, but Chase returned within minutes. He was alone, and his face was grim. He sat down across from her.

"Mandy's boss was in the kitchen," he said in a monotone. "She confirms that Mandy hasn't had a day off since she started three weeks ago."

"Then she's lying, too!" Kelly cried.

"She showed me her ledger," Chase said. "She keeps a record of how many hours her employees work for payroll purposes. Mandy's name was on every page."

"Then she falsified it. I'm telling you, Chase. They're both lying." Kelly bit her lip, wondering how she could convince him. Then it hit her. If Toby was also a kidnap victim as she suspected, then the police would be forced to take her claim seriously. "What about Toby?"

"What about him?"

"Did you ask her about custody?"

"I did," he said.

"And?"

"And I'm pretty sure she's going to give it to me. She even told me his real name is Toby Johnson, not Toby Smith. You were right about Mandy running from her father. He was in jail for assaulting her."

The hope in his face was so palpable Kelly hated to dash it. In a perfect world, there wouldn't be any impediment to Chase being awarded custody of the boy. In a perfect world, what Kelly and Chase had begun last night would turn into something beautiful and lasting. Then Toby would have two parents instead of one.

But the world was far from perfect.

"I doubt Mandy has the authority to give you custody, Chase," she said.

"Because you think Toby's a kidnapped child, too."

She nodded, feeling unutterably sad.

"Mandy claims he isn't," Chase said.

"Of course she'd say that. Why would she tell the truth about Toby when she lied about the child she kidnapped in Utica?"

"She says she has proof that Toby isn't kidnapped."

Before Kelly could ask what kind of proof, Mandy strode through the restaurant with some sort of document in hand.

"Here it is." She laid the paper on the table with a flourish. At the top was the seal of Pennsylvania. It was a birth certificate, Kelly realized. Her heart began a slow, painful thump. Happiness over what this could mean for Chase and Toby warred with despair.

Chase picked up the birth certificate and read it over, then gazed at Kelly with unreadable eyes and handed it to her. The father's name was listed as unknown, but the blanks were filled in for the mother's name and the baby's name:

Amanda Elizabeth Johnson and Toby Aaron Johnson.

Mandy jerked her head toward Kelly. "I told you she was lying."

"Why would I do that?" Kelly asked dazedly, a last-ditch attempt to convince Chase she was telling the truth. "Why would I spend all this time looking for you if I was lying?"

"I'll tell you why," Mandy said. "Because you're in

a heap of trouble you want to pin on somebody else. Who better than a woman who looks just like you?"

The explanation sounded credible even to Kelly. Chase said nothing.

It was patently obvious that Kelly had reached the end of her trail. Nobody was going to believe she'd been a victim of mistaken identity.

Not Chase.

Not her lawyer.

Not the cops who arrested her.

And especially not the district attorney who was prepared to prosecute her.

Even if Kelly could get somebody to reexamine the case, the bottom line would come down to the testimony of the eyewitnesses.

Now that Mandy had cut and bleached her hair, nobody would ever confuse the two of them. Even Kelly knew she looked more like the woman with the shoulder-length brown hair who'd snatched the child than the kidnapper did herself.

CHAPTER FOURTEEN

TOYS LITTERED THE FAMILY ROOM at the Bradford house, but Toby wasn't paying attention to any of them. He batted at Kelly's nose as if it was a plaything, an unfortunate habit of which she'd been trying to break him.

Now she wouldn't get the chance.

"No, sweetie." She gently but firmly took hold of his wrist. "That hurts."

Not true. She couldn't feel much of anything. The blow from her failed quest for justice had left her numb.

"The little scamp must already be feeling better." Charlie came up beside where she sat with Toby on the overstuffed sofa and touched the child's forehead. "Yep. The fever's gone. It was just a mild ear infection, like the doc said."

When Kelly and Chase had returned from Fox Tail less than a half hour before, Toby had crawled over to her and wordlessly asked to be picked up. He'd been content to let her hold him since, almost as though he sensed their time together was short.

"Did you run into any trouble filling out those forms at the doctor's office?" Chase asked his father. He'd already changed into his uniform and stood in the family room, feet a shoulder's width apart, impatient to get going.

"A bunch. I left most things blank and said I needed to check with you," Charlie said. "Thank God we'll be able to provide complete information now."

They hadn't told Charlie everything that had happened in Fox Tail, but he knew they'd found Mandy and she'd agreed to sign over custody of Toby.

"Mandy called the pediatrician she used in Harrisburg and authorized him to send Toby's records," Chase said. "She also gave me his birth certificate."

The very document that proved Toby wasn't a kidnapping victim—and cast grave doubt on the fact that his mother was a criminal.

"I'll be back around six, no later than seven." Chase nodded to his father and planted his customary kiss on the top of Toby's head before addressing Kelly. "We'll talk then."

He seemed to take her agreement for granted because he left the room in a hurry, the door closing behind him moments later.

Kelly swallowed, but her throat still felt clogged.

She had spent most of the drive back from Fox Tail staring out the passenger-side window, barely taking note of the lush greens of the summer mountains. She and Chase had done very little talking, although he had asked her the time of her preliminary hearing and expressed approval that it was scheduled for early afternoon the next day, saying, "We'll leave by seven so we can get there by noon." It seemed Chase meant to deliver her personally to the courtroom.

"What are you and Chase going to talk about?" Charlie asked, referring back to Chase's cryptic parting comment.

She started to say it was nothing important, but Charlie regarded her with such concern that tears pricked her eyes. She dashed them away, annoyed at herself.

"Oh, Charlie," she said. "I thought everything would be okay when we found Mandy but it's not. And the worst part is Chase doesn't believe me."

He was instantly at her side, taking Toby from her and putting him down beside his toys. Then he sat beside her and gave her his full attention.

"Now tell me what you're talking about," he said.

The story poured from her like water from a tap. She started with her real name and told him about the day she'd stumbled across Mandy and the kidnapped child in the park. He didn't interrupt, letting her tell the tale at her own pace.

She owned up to all her lies, refusing to justify them. The only part of the story she left out was what had happened between her and Chase the night before, but Charlie had probably figured out how she felt about Chase on his own.

"What did you mean about Chase not believing you?" he asked when she finished talking.

"I can't really blame him, Charlie. Mandy was very convincing. She even had an alibi."

"Then she was lying," he said. "Chase should know that girl lies like a rug."

"Unfortunately, I do, too," she said.

"That's different."

"Not so different," she said sadly. "Now I'm like that

boy who cried wolf. I'm telling the truth, but nobody believes me."

"I believe you," he said staunchly. "What are you going to do next?"

"I'm going back to Wenona for my hearing," she said. "I can't live my life on the run. I'll tell the police about Mandy and try to get them to investigate, but I don't have much hope of that happening."

"When is your hearing?"

"Tomorrow afternoon." She released a shuddering breath. "Can I ask you a favor, Charlie?"

"Anything."

"Can you take me someplace where I can rent a car?"

She heard him exhale. "Why?"

"Because I have to do this on my own. Chase wants to drive me to Wenona tomorrow, but I couldn't bear to have him hovering over me, making sure I do the right thing."

Charlie's lower lip jutted forward. "You don't know that's why he wants to go with you."

"I know what he's like, Charlie. So do you. He's the reason you aren't with Teresa."

Charlie recoiled as if she'd struck him in a particularly sore spot. She regretted his pain but she'd spoken the truth.

"That didn't come out right." She thought about how to phrase what she wanted to say. "You told me once that Chase always tries to do what's right. I have charges against me. Of course he wants to make sure I show up for my hearing."

"But you're innocent!"

Her throat grew thick. "You're the first one who's believed me since I got arrested."

"I shouldn't be the first," he muttered. "I should sit that son of mine down and give him a talking to."

"Please don't, Charlie." She put a hand on his arm. "I don't want him to believe me only because you tell him he should."

"But he should!"

She had to smile at that. "Like I said, it's good to have you on my side. Now about that car-rental place. Will you take me?"

IT TURNED OUT THAT THE nearest place to rent a car was at a dealership forty-five minutes away. Charlie stood by her while she filled out the paperwork, Toby on his hip.

"I'll take care of the bill," he said when she got out her credit card. He handed over Toby and pulled out his own wallet before she had a chance to protest. "I won't take no for an answer. I just wish I could do more."

After the paperwork was filled out, she transferred her backpack from the trunk of Charlie's car to the rental. The only thing left was to leave.

She'd thought she had said goodbye to Toby and Charlie once already at the bed-and-breakfast. This time was different. This time Charlie knew it was farewell, too. Even Toby seemed to sense it. He started to bat at her nose, then stopped and stroked her face instead.

"You're a good boy, sweetheart." She kissed his baby-soft cheek, smelled his clean scent and felt an ache in her chest. "I'm going to miss you."

She tried to hand Toby over to Charlie, but the baby clung to her, his face starting to crumple.

"Don't cry, sweetie," she said in a low, soothing voice. "Everything will be all right."

"He doesn't want you to go, either," Charlie said.

"I have to go." She was finally successful in handing over Toby, but he looked seriously unhappy. She kissed Charlie on the cheek, tenderness welling inside her chest. In a few short days, she'd come to love this man like a father. "Thanks for being such a good friend."

"What should I tell Chase?" he asked.

The tears she'd been fighting threatened, but she held them back. Tell him I love him, she thought. Tell him I wish he'd found it in his heart to believe me.

"Tell him not to worry. I won't skip the hearing."

She'd show up in the courtroom at the scheduled time, just as Chase would want her to. Even if it meant spending the next year in prison.

CHARLIE STOOD UNOBSERVED AT the gate that led to the backyard of the big house where Teresa had lived with her husband and children.

She hunched over in the portion of the once-large vegetable garden she'd continued to tend, fingering a tomato that wasn't quite ripe. The sun bathed her in light. Even in an oversize shirt and stained khaki shorts, he thought she was beautiful.

Beautiful and stubborn and maddening.

But if she wasn't all those things, she wouldn't be Teresa.

He unhooked the latch on the gate and pushed it open. It creaked. Teresa's chin rose, and their eyes met across the expanse of yard.

She stood up, brushing her hands on her shorts. She did not look surprised to see him. "Hello, Charlie."

"Hello, Teresa."

Her eyes widened. "That's it? No, 'Hello, gorgeous'? Or 'Who let you out of heaven?'"

"I'm not that corny," Charlie said.

"Yes," Teresa said, "you are."

"Not today I'm not," Charlie said firmly. "Today we have things to talk about."

After he'd seen Kelly off and put Toby down for his afternoon nap, his mind had been consumed with Teresa. Not surprising since he'd thought of little else since the for-sale sign had gone up in front of her house.

He'd initially planned to bring Toby along on this visit and had even written a note to Chase on the grease-board to that effect, but then he'd spotted Judy Allen outside with her kids and asked if she'd watch him.

The things Charlie had to say were better said without Toby distracting him.

"It won't make any difference, but by all means, let's talk," Teresa said.

She bent down and picked up three ripe tomatoes she'd set aside, then led him to her back porch. It was a simple structure, little more than a painted cement slab covered by an awning, but she'd made it pretty by hanging baskets of colorful flowers and covering the wrought iron chairs with patterned seat cushions. She put the tomatoes on a round table, then sat down herself, waving a hand in silent invitation for him to do the same.

By not inviting him into the house, he suspected she

was trying to drive home the point that they were already through.

His stomach lurched, the prospect making him too nervous to sit. He leaned against the porch railing.

"If you came to try to talk me out of selling the house, save your breath." Her chin had a stubborn lift, but her mouth sagged, as though she wasn't quite as in control as she'd like him to believe. The droop gave him hope.

"I think you should sell," he said.

"What?" She looked more shocked than if he'd told her to burn down the place.

"You should sell," he repeated. "Look around. It's way too much house for one person."

She jumped up from her chair and crossed to where he stood, placing her hands on her hips. "This is one of your tricks, isn't it?"

"I don't know what you mean."

"You're agreeing with me, even though you don't agree so I'll take up the argument you should have made."

"Huh?"

"Don't you tell me that you think it's a good idea for me to move away from all my friends and the town I love."

"I don't," Charlie said.

She took her hands off her hips and threw them into the air. "You just said you did!"

"I said you should sell your house, not move away from town," he clarified.

"You're not making sense, Charlie Bradford." Her eyes flashed. "If I sold my house but stayed in town, where would I live?"

He swallowed and straightened from the railing, cut-ting the distance between them to not more than a foot or two. "With me."

"With you?" She looked well and truly confused. And just maybe, a little bit hopeful.

What the heck, he thought, and dropped to one knee. Once his knee was touching the porch, though, his throat swelled with emotion.

"Are you doing what I think you're doing?" she whispered.

He cleared his throat. "Only if you think I'm asking you to marry me."

She promptly burst into tears. He straightened, damning his creaky knees for not moving faster. His leg bumped the table, knocking a few tomatoes to the cement floor in the process, but he paid them no mind. He took her beloved face in his hands. The tears streaming down her cheeks could have been staining his own face. He couldn't believe their romance would end this way but neither could he bear to see her so sad.

"Don't cry, sweetheart," he said. "I know Andrea and your grandchildren need you. I won't make you choose."

The tears flowed harder, but she managed to choke out between tears, "Yes."

"If you have your heart set on Philadelphia…" He stopped, gaped at her. "What did you say?"

"Yes," she said, sniffling but smiling. "I said yes. I'll marry you."

He wasn't sure who moved first, but suddenly they were wrapped in each other's arms, their lips locked, their hearts touching. He smoothed her hair back from her face, caressing her cheeks, her lips, her nose, his fingers coming away damp with her tears.

"I don't even have a ring," he said. "What kind of a proposal was that without a ring?"

"A wonderful proposal." Her watery smile was the most gorgeous thing he'd ever seen. "I don't need a ring. I only need you."

"Now who sounds corny?" he asked, and she laughed. He kissed her again, more lingeringly this time, drawing back only because there were things they hadn't yet discussed, matters to be decided. Yet he found he couldn't let her go, not when he'd come so close to losing her.

"Have you told Chase?" she asked.

"Not yet. I didn't know myself what I was going to say until I got over here."

Her expression changed. She extricated herself from his arms and put a few paces between them. "Then how could you ask me to marry you?"

"I asked you to marry me because I love you," he said. "And you love me. Otherwise you wouldn't have said yes."

"Of course I love you," she said. "But Chase's reaction could be too big an obstacle for us to overcome."

"I won't let it be," he said stubbornly. "It took that for-sale sign for me to realize what was important. I'll make him understand."

"You still should have told Chase before you asked me," she said.

"Told me what?"

Charlie turned to see his son standing at the foot of

the porch. It was obvious he'd come through the open gate to the backyard, but it was less clear how long he'd been there.

Teresa said nothing, but it wasn't her responsibility to break the news to his son. It was Charlie's.

His stomach tightened at what was to come. He loathed hurting his son, but he couldn't give up Teresa.

"Told you that Teresa and I love each other." Charlie moved closer to her, presenting a united front. "We started seeing each other a few months ago."

"Seeing each other?" Chase struggled for words. "Mom just died."

"We know the timing's not great, and it doesn't change the way we felt about your mother," Charlie said. "We both loved her. We both miss her. But we can't bring her back."

"Dad, she hasn't even been dead a year!" Chase rasped out the words.

"Teresa and I didn't plan what happened. It just did."

"Not even a year, Dad!"

Charlie realized now he'd never felt disloyal to his late wife. Only to Chase.

"In a lot of ways, you're just like your mother," Charlie said, "but you're acting like an ass."

"What!"

"An ass," Charlie repeated. "I knew your mother better than anybody. She'd want me to be happy again. She'd want Teresa to be happy. She wouldn't keep some damn schedule about when it's okay to love again."

Chase opened his mouth to speak, then closed it again.

"I asked Teresa to marry me," Charlie went on. "She said yes. We'd like your blessing, but we'll get married without it." Charlie took Teresa's hand and found that it was trembling. "I can't keep hurting Teresa because of you."

"Because of me?"

"Charlie didn't want you to find out about us, but I refused to keep sneaking around." Teresa spoke for the first time since Chase had showed up. "I was going to move to Philadelphia."

"Because of me," Chase said, but this time it wasn't a question. It was a statement. He rubbed a hand over the back of his neck, then met Charlie's eyes. "I hate that you felt you couldn't tell me."

"I hate that you can't wish us well," Charlie said.

"Whoa! I never said that."

"So you're okay with us getting married?" Teresa asked.

He hesitated, and Charlie could see emotions chasing across his son's face. He thought he read grief and resistance but couldn't be sure what else.

"You'll have to give me time to get used to the idea, but I should be able to manage it," Chase said slowly, with difficulty. He looked at Teresa. "I already think of you as family."

Charlie's heart felt like it was filled with helium. He let go of Teresa's hand and wrapped his son in a hearty bear hug. Teresa excused herself to go mop up her tears, but Charlie suspected she was giving them time alone.

"This means a lot to me, son." Charlie heard the catch in his voice and decided it was time to lighten the mood. "But I don't think you should start calling her Mother Teresa."

The corners of Chase's mouth lifted. He hadn't completely adjusted to the idea of his father remarrying, Charlie thought, but he'd get there.

"I haven't even told her she's going to be Grandmother Teresa to Toby yet," he said. "Everything happened too fast."

"Where are Toby and Kelly anyway? After I saw your note, I thought I'd find all three of you here."

Charlie had been so caught up in how Chase would react to his new romance that he'd forgotten that Chase had been equally disapproving of Kelly. He stiffened. "Toby's with Judy Allen and her kids. Kelly's probably back in Wenona by now."

"Back in Wenona!" The tone of Chase's voice spiked. "But we were supposed to drive up there together tomorrow morning."

"She told me." Charlie didn't try to keep the displeasure from his voice. "She also told me about the kidnapping charge and her hearing. I can't say I blame her for leaving town."

"How could she leave town without a car?" Chase seemed visibly upset, but Charlie couldn't muster any sympathy for him.

"I rented her a car." Charlie scowled at Chase. "She said to tell you not to worry about her showing up for the hearing. She'll be there even without a watchdog."

"A watchdog?" Chase shook his head. "But I don't understand. Why didn't she tell me she was leaving?"

Thinking back over the last fifteen minutes and his own reluctance to confide in Chase, Charlie cocked a brow. "Do you really have to ask?"

CHAPTER FIFTEEN

"WHERE HAVE YOU BEEN?" Kelly's lawyer demanded the instant they were in the austere downtown Wenona law offices of Bergman and Dietz and behind closed doors. "Do you know how many messages I left you?"

"Ten." She hadn't deleted the messages she'd checked remotely and had counted them last night when she arrived home. Spencer Yates had left one message on her answering machine for every day she'd been gone.

Had it really only been ten days? It seemed impossible to fall in love over ten short days, but the persistent ache in her chest said otherwise.

She could attribute the dull pain to a seemingly inevitable prison sentence that would strip her of her teaching career and chance to adopt a child.

Except any of those eventualities would be a little easier to face if only Chase had believed her.

"Ten!" Yates said. "That's right. Ten messages! And you didn't answer any of them!"

"That's not true." Kelly crossed her legs at the ankles, trying to give the false impression that she was in total control. "I called your office last night to agree to meet with you before the hearing."

"You called after office hours when you knew nobody would be here!" Yates said.

"I'm sorry."

"Where have you been?"

She met his eyes. "I was looking for the real kidnapper."

His brows rose slightly, and she knew he was as skeptical that such a person existed as the first time they'd met. "And did you find her?"

"As a matter of fact, I did." Kelly dug into her purse and pulled out a sheet of paper on which she'd written Mandy's name and the address of the Dancing Turtle. She handed it to him. "I'd like you to pass this on to the police and get the hearing postponed."

He held up the paper. "Is this legit?"

"Yes. Mandy Johnson kidnapped that baby, not me."

He glanced at the paper again. "I assume you have more than just this name and address? What proof do you have that this woman is the kidnapper?"

Kelly's new policy of being honest all the time, no matter what the fallout, kicked in. "No other proof. Mandy insists she didn't kidnap anyone. She even has someone giving her an alibi, so it's their word against mine."

He didn't sigh, but his chest heaved up and down as though he was holding one back. "And you honestly think this is worth pursuing?"

"Yes, I do," Kelly said firmly. "She's the kidnapper. I'm innocent."

Yates squeezed the bridge of his nose, then balanced his elbows on his desk and leaned forward. "I'd be remiss as your lawyer if I didn't explain what could happen if we request a postponement."

"Go on," Kelly said when he paused.

"The plea bargain I worked out isn't good forever. If this goes nowhere, the DA could get seriously annoyed. He could take the offer off the table just like that." He snapped his fingers. "It's a very good offer."

"On the phone, you said I'd have to serve a year in prison."

"I've told you this before, but it bears repeating. If the case goes to trial and you're convicted of second-degree kidnapping, you could be sentenced for up to eight years. Luckily for you, everyone seems convinced this incident was brought on by stress over your infertility. That's why the DA reduced the charge to endangering the welfare of a child and stipulated you submit to ongoing counseling."

Kelly looked left, then right, but there was no way out of this mess. "So I'm supposed to get treatment for a problem I don't have and plead guilty to a crime I didn't commit?"

"You can plead no contest." Yates removed his elbows from the desk and sat back in his chair. "It's the same as a guilty plea in the eyes of the law, but the plea can't be used against you in a civil case."

Her stomach cramped. "Are you advising me to take the deal?"

"I'm presenting the facts as I know them so you can make an informed decision."

The intercom on his desk buzzed, followed by the voice of his secretary. "You'll want to take this call, Mr. Yates."

"Excuse me," he told Kelly before punching a button, picking up the phone and angling his chair away from her.

The decision she had to make crowded her brain, drowning out Yates's side of the conversation. Could she really gamble years of her life on the authorities believing her instead of Mandy Johnson? Even Chase didn't believe her.

Then again, could she give up her hopes and dreams without a fight? No school system would hire a woman who'd done time for child endangerment, and no adoption agency would approve her. Not to mention that pleading no contest would be tantamount to lying and she'd promised herself never to lie again.

Yates hung up the phone and turned to face her.

"No!" she said without preamble. "I won't admit to something I didn't do."

Yates nodded to the phone, a shocked expression on his lean face. "You probably won't have to. The DA is going to ask for a continuance."

"What? Why?"

"New evidence, the DA's office says. The continuance is just a formality. It seems the DA expects all charges against you to be dropped."

Kelly's hands flew to her face. "I don't understand."

"Neither do I," he said. "We'll find out the details at the hearing. You will be there, right?"

"Of course I'll be there," Kelly said.

"I'll see you then." He looked down at the papers on his desk, and Kelly realized she'd been dismissed.

She walked out of his office, through the building and

into the late-morning sun. She breathed deeply of the warm, sweet air, the same way she had that morning after spending the night in jail. But even though her long nightmare seemed to be reaching an end, euphoria wouldn't come.

Not when the man she loved was back in Indigo Springs, believing the worst of her.

Five wide steps led from the law office to a small city park, complete with benches and a pretty fountain. When she reached level ground, she looked up.

There, beside the fountain, was Chase.

CHASE'S FEET FELT AS THOUGH they were encased in plaster. He'd intended to go to Kelly the instant she emerged from the law office, but confusion and uncertainty froze him in place. She hadn't looked happy, even before she spotted him, and that didn't make sense.

Keeping her head high, she walked toward him at a quick clip. She looked lovely in high heels and a summery-patterned dress suitable for court. She also looked remote and unapproachable. He met her halfway, wishing he could turn back the clock and redo the last twenty-four hours.

"It wasn't necessary for you to come all this way." Her speech was stiff and formal. "I never planned to skip the hearing."

Chase winced. Did she really think him so intractable he'd drive hundreds of miles to assure the system had a chance to treat her unjustly?

Of course she did, he admitted to himself.

"That's not why I'm here," he said.

She stiffened her shoulders. "How did you find me anyway?"

"I went to your apartment first. When you weren't there, I called the courthouse and got the name of your attorney. I took a chance you'd come to see him."

She looked seriously displeased, as though she hadn't even heard him deny he was in Wenona to make sure she attended the hearing.

"Excuse me. I have to be in court in a few hours," she said briskly and moved to get past him.

"Did your attorney tell you the DA's going to ask for a continuance?"

She paused in the act of sidestepping him. "How did you know that?"

She held herself rigidly, her body language communicating that she didn't want him to touch her. He didn't blame her. He nodded toward a bench that overlooked the fountain. "Sit with me."

At first he thought she might refuse, but then she marched to the bench and sat, careful to keep distance between them. A couple with a little girl about two years old sat down on a nearby bench. The girl toddled up to the fountain and dragged a hand through the water, laughing when it splashed into her face.

It was entirely his fault Kelly thought he believed her capable of kidnapping a child not much younger than the little girl, Chase thought.

"My buddy Dave has a brother-in-law who's a police detective in northeast Pennsylvania," he began. "After we got back from Fox Tail yesterday, I got his phone number and called him."

"Why?"

"Because something about Mandy's alibi was fishy. You didn't meet the restaurant owner, but she seemed nervous. So I got Dave's brother-in-law to pay her a visit."

She angled her body toward him, her eyes wide and questioning. He could smell her shampoo and the scent that was uniquely hers. He clenched his fist to stop from reaching for her.

"It turned out Mandy had worked at the restaurant only for a week. She and the owner are old friends— that's why Mandy had the T-shirt. When Mandy found out a woman called the restaurant asking for her, she asked her friend to lie about how long she'd been working there."

"Did the restaurant owner know about the kidnapping?"

"Not the real story. Mandy told her you'd committed a crime and were trying to blame Mandy because you two look alike."

Kelly shifted, her expression puzzled. "The restaurant owner retracting the alibi doesn't seem like enough evidence to get the hearing postponed."

"It wasn't. I got a call on the drive up here. Dave's brother-in-law questioned Mandy this morning, and given what the restaurant owner said, Mandy admitted that she'd lied. That she'd manufactured her alibi. So he had enough to contact the Wenona cops. Once they showed up and started asking her some tough questions, she folded and all but confessed. They're extraditing her to New York as soon as possible."

Kelly put a hand to her head, finding it hard to absorb

what he was saying. When Spencer Yates had told her the charges against her would probably be dropped, she hadn't fully believed him. Mandy's capture changed everything.

"But why would she do it? Why would she take that baby?" It was the question that had bothered her from the start, the one that seemed so unanswerable she'd almost pled no contest to a crime she hadn't committed.

"Apparently she just lost it," Chase said. "The baby reminded her of Toby, so the detective thinks she snatched him to prove she could be a good parent. It didn't take her long to realize she didn't want to take care of the kidnapped baby any more than she had Toby. That's where you came in."

"The wrong place at the wrong time," Kelly said.

"That about sums it up," Chase said. "The detective fully expects her to face charges."

The charges Kelly had barely escaped. Charges that might have landed her in prison if not for Chase.

"You believed me." The knowledge slowly dawned on her and filled her with awe. "You believed me when I told you I hadn't kidnapped anyone."

"I didn't want to believe you because it meant admitting Toby might also have been kidnapped," he said. "But, yes, I believed you."

"But...but then why didn't you say something after Mandy gave you Toby's birth certificate? In the car, on the way back to Indigo Springs, you hardly said a word."

"I was trying to make sense of it all. If Mandy wanted a baby, all she had to do was come back for Toby. I couldn't figure out why she would lie or why her boss would lie for her." He shifted, looking uncomfortable. "Her story was credible—and yours wasn't."

He seemed to be talking in riddles. "So you didn't believe me until that detective told you Mandy's story had fallen apart?"

He shook his head vehemently. "That's not true. I believed you way before then." He paused. "I was just trying to figure out *why* I believed you."

The apprehension in his voice alerted her that the conclusion he'd reached was vital.

"Did you figure it out?" she asked softly.

"Oh, yeah," he said, then took her hand and looked into her eyes. "I love you, Kelly. That's why I believed you."

Her pulse raced even faster than it had when the cops had arrested her. Her breath caught, making it difficult to draw in air, but she seemed unable to do anything except stare at him.

He wore slacks, a blue dress shirt and a tie. He should have looked professional, but the garments were wrinkled from his long drive to Wenona and his hair appeared as though he'd been running his fingers through it. He looked endearingly nervous.

"You don't have to say anything right now." Chase said, his hand tightening on hers. "I know we haven't known each other for long and that you might have a tough time forgiving me. I know I'm a self-righteous jerk, but all I want is a chance."

She managed to breathe again because there was something she really needed to tell him. "I don't think you're a self-righteous jerk."

He cocked an eyebrow. "Are you sure about that?"

"Very sure," she said, smiling tremulously at him, "because I wouldn't have fallen in love with a self-righteous jerk."

"You love me?"

"You and Toby and Charlie, too." She felt tears forming in her eyes. "Most of all, you."

She reached for him at the same time he wrapped her in his arms, eliciting a warm, allover feeling she recognized for what it was: Love.

She kissed him, letting the feeling sweep over her, knowing perhaps for the first time in her life exactly what she wanted.

She wanted Chase.

A long while later he broke off the kiss, still keeping her in his arms, his eyes earnest. "You didn't let me finish apologizing."

A corner of her mouth lifted. "I already told you I don't think you're a self-righteous jerk."

"But I am, to quote my father, an ass."

"When did Charlie call you that?"

"When he told me he was going to marry Teresa whether I liked it or not."

Good for Charlie, Kelly thought. "What did you say?"

"I didn't react too well. But then Teresa said my dad had been afraid to tell me, and I realized I'd caused them a lot of pain." He paused. "Just like I caused you pain. You felt you couldn't tell me the truth, either. I'm sorry for that."

"And I'm sorry for lying to you," she said. "I won't do it again."

"Again? Does that mean you see a future for us?" He

leaned closer to her, as though he was hanging on her answer. "You told me before that you love Indigo Springs. Do you love it enough to move there?"

She reached up and stroked his face. "I love *you* enough to move to Indigo Springs."

"I won't rush you," Chase promised. "I'll wine you and dine you and do my best to make you forget I ever doubted you. But I should warn you I have a kid who needs a mother. So be aware that, down the line, I'm the marrying kind."

The little girl and her parents were leaving the park. The child walked between the adults, holding each of their hands as she skipped along. They looked like a happy family, but no more content than Kelly vowed she'd be with the Bradford men.

She smiled at him, amazed that her journey to clear her name had brought her to this happy place.

"The marrying kind," she repeated. "So am I."

* * * * *

Don't miss Darlene Gardner's next
RETURN TO INDIGO SPRINGS *novel,*
Superromance #1580
THE SECRET SIN
Available August 2009!

*In honor of our 60th anniversary,
Harlequin® American Romance®
is celebrating by featuring an all-American male
each month, all year long with*
MEN MADE IN AMERICA!
*This June, we'll be featuring American men living
in the West.*

Here's a sneak preview of
THE CHIEF RANGER
by Rebecca Winters.

*Chief Ranger Vance Rossiter has to confront the sister
of a man who died while under Vance's watch...and
also confront his attraction to her.*

"Chief Ranger Rossiter?" The sight of the woman who'd stepped inside Vance's office brought him to his feet. "I'm Rachel Darrow. Your secretary said I should come right in."

"Please," he said, walking around his desk to shake her hand. At a glance he estimated she was in her mid-twenties. Her feminine curves did wonders for the pale blue T-shirt and jeans she was wearing. "Ranger Jarvis informed me there's a young boy with you."

The unfriendly expression in her beautiful green eyes caught him off guard. "Yes," was her clipped reply. "When we arrived in Yosemite, the ranger told me I couldn't go anywhere in the park until I talked to you first."

"That's right."

"Knowing you wanted this meeting to be private, he offered to show my nephew around Headquarters."

So this woman was the victim's sister… "What's his name?"

"Nicky."

The boy who haunted Vance's dreams now had a name. "How old is he?"

"He turned six three weeks ago. Were you the man in charge when my brother and sister-in-law were killed?"

"Yes. To tell you I'm sorry for what happened couldn't begin to convey my feelings."

The woman's gaze didn't flicker. "I won't even try to describe mine. Just tell me one thing. Was their accident preventable?"

"Yes," he answered without hesitation.

"In other words, the people working under you fell asleep on your watch and two lives were snuffed out as a result."

Hearing it put like that, he had to set the record straight. "My staff had nothing to do with it. I, myself, could have prevented the loss of life."

Ms. Darrow's expression hardened. "So you admit culpability."

"Yes. I take full blame."

A look of pain crossed over her features. "You can just stand there and admit it?" Her cry echoed that of his own tortured soul.

"Yes." He sucked in his breath.

"I work for a cruise line. Aboard ship, it's the captain's responsibility to maintain rigid safety regulations. If a disaster like that had happened while he was in charge, he would have been relieved of his command and never given another ship again."

Rachel Darrow couldn't know she was preaching to the converted. "If you've come to the park with the intention of bringing a lawsuit against me for negligence, maybe you should." It would only be what he deserved.

"Maybe I will."

In the next instant, she wheeled around and hurried out of his office. Vance could have gone after her, but it would cause a scene, something he was loath to do for a variety of reasons. In the first place, he needed to cool down before he approached her again.

The discovery of the Darrows' frozen bodies had affected every ranger in the park. A little boy had been orphaned—a boy whose aunt was all he had left.

* * * * *

Will Rachel allow Vance to explain—
and will she let him into her heart?
Find out in
THE CHIEF RANGER
Available June 2009
from Harlequin® American Romance®.

HARLEQUIN
60 YEARS
of pure reading pleasure®

We'll be spotlighting a different series every month
throughout 2009 to celebrate our 60th anniversary.

Look for Harlequin®
American Romance® in June!

Join us for a year-long celebration of the rugged
American male! From cops to cowboys—
Men Made in America has the hero
you've been dreaming about!

MEN
Made in America
American ★ Romance

Look for

The Chief Ranger

by Rebecca Winters, on sale in June!

HARLEQUIN® *Romance*®

Escape Around the World
Dream destinations, whirlwind weddings!

Honeymoon with the Boss
by
JESSICA HART

Top tycoon Tom Maddison is used to calling the shots—until his convenient marriage falls through. But rather than waste his honeymoon, he'll take his boardroom to the beach and bring his oh-so-sensible secretary Imogen on a tropical business trip! But will Tom finally see the sexy woman that prudent Imogen truly is?

Available in June wherever books are sold.

www.eHarlequin.com   HRI75900

REQUEST YOUR FREE BOOKS!

2 FREE NOVELS PLUS 2 FREE GIFTS!

HARLEQUIN®

Super Romance®

Exciting, emotional, unexpected!

YES! Please send me 2 FREE Harlequin® Superromance® novels and my 2 FREE gifts (gifts are worth about $10). After receiving them, if I don't wish to receive any more books, I can return the shipping statement marked "cancel." If I don't cancel, I will receive 6 brand-new novels every month and be billed just $4.69 per book in the U.S. or $5.24 per book in Canada. That's a savings of close to 15% off the cover price! It's quite a bargain! Shipping and handling is just 50¢ per book*. I understand that accepting the 2 free books and gifts places me under no obligation to buy anything. I can always return a shipment and cancel at any time. Even if I never buy another book from Harlequin, the two free books and gifts are mine to keep forever.

135 HDN EYLG 336 HDN EYLS

Name	(PLEASE PRINT)	

Address		Apt. #

City	State/Prov.	Zip/Postal Code

Signature (if under 18, a parent or guardian must sign)

Mail to the **Harlequin Reader Service:**

IN U.S.A.: P.O. Box 1867, Buffalo, NY 14240-1867
IN CANADA: P.O. Box 609, Fort Erie, Ontario L2A 5X3

Not valid to current subscribers of Harlequin Superromance books.

**Are you a current subscriber of Harlequin Superromance books
and want to receive the larger-print edition?
Call 1-800-873-8635 today!**

* Terms and prices subject to change without notice. Prices do not include applicable taxes Sales tax applicable in N.Y. Canadian residents will be charged applicable provincial taxes and GST. Offer not valid in Quebec. This offer is limited to one order per household. All orders subject to approval. Credit or debit balances in a customer's account(s) may be offset by any other outstanding balance owed by or to the customer. Please allow 4 to 6 weeks for delivery. Offer available while quantities last.

Your Privacy: Harlequin is committed to protecting your privacy. Our Privacy Policy is available online at www.eHarlequin.com or upon request from the Reader Service. From time to time we make our lists of customers available to reputable third parties who may have a product or service of interest to you. If you would prefer we not share your name and address, please check here. ☐

HSx

You're invited to join our Tell Harlequin Reader Panel!

By joining our new reader panel you will:

- Receive Harlequin® books—they are FREE and yours to keep with no obligation to purchase anything!
- Participate in fun online surveys
- Exchange opinions and ideas with women just like you
- Have a say in our new book ideas and help us publish the best in women's fiction

In addition, you will have a chance to win great prizes and receive special gifts! See Web site for details. Some conditions apply. Space is limited.

To join, visit us at
www.TellHarlequin.com.

COMING NEXT MONTH

Available June 9, 2009

#1566 A SMALL-TOWN HOMECOMING • Terry McLaughlin
Built to Last
The return of architect Tess Roussel to her hometown has put her on a collision
course with John Jameson Quinn. The contractor has her reeling…his scandalous
overshadows everything. Tess wants to believe that the contractor is deserving of h
professional admiration and her trust, but her love, too?

#1567 A HOLIDAY ROMANCE • Carrie Alexander
A summer holiday in the desert? What had Alice Potter been thinking? If it wasn't
resort manager Kyle Jarreau, her dream vacation would be a nightmare. But can th
keep their fling a secret…? For Kyle's sake, they *have* to.

#1568 FROM FRIEND TO FATHER • Tracy Wolff
Reece Sandler never planned to raise his daughter with Sarah Martin. They were c
friends when he agreed to be his surrogate. Now things have changed and they ha
be parents—together. Fine. Easy. But only if Reece can control his attraction to Sa

#1569 BEST FOR THE BABY • Ann Evans
9 Months Later
Pregnant and alone, Alaina Tillman returns to Lake Harmony and Zack Davidson,
girlhood love. Yet as attracted as she is to him, life isn't just about the two of them
anymore. She has to do what's best for her baby. Does that mean letting Zack in—
pushing him away?

#1570 NO ORDINARY COWBOY• Mary Sullivan
Home on the Ranch
A ranch is so not Amy Graves's scene. Still, she promised to help, so here she is.
thing is she starts to feel at home. And even funnier, she starts to fall for a cowboy
Hank Shelter. As she soon discovers, however, there's nothing ordinary about him

#1571 ALL THAT LOVE IS • Ginger Chambers
Everlasting Love
Jillian Davis was prepared to walk away from her marriage. But when her husban
Brad, takes her on a shortcut, an accident nearly kills them. Now, with the SUV a
their fragile shelter, Jillian's only hope lies with the man she was ready to leave b
forever.…

HSRCNMBPA05